WHEN THEY DO

WHEN THEY DO

SARA BELLCAMP

Zeta Indie Publishing

Contents

1   Marco and Nina Go Steady   1

2   Marco and Nina Have a Party   10

3   Marco and Nina Get a Cat   17

4   Marco and Nina Move in Together   28

5   Marco and Nina's New Year's Eve   42

6   Marco and Nina's Engagement Party   54

7   Marco and Nina's Wedding Registry   62

8   Marco and Nina's Week Of   74

9   Nina's Bachelorette Party   86

10   Marco's Bachelor Party   96

11   Marco and Nina's Rehearsal Dinner   107

12   Marco and Nina's Wedding   119

About The Author   133

I

Marco and Nina Go Steady

This story is not about me. It's about Marco and Nina.

I wasn't even there when it started.

Don't get me wrong. I lead a superbly fantastic life. I'm even somewhat of a legend in some circles. Alex Keaton—tall, dark, handsome, always impeccably dressed, suit and tie, built like your typical Greek god.

You've probably already heard of me. A different girl every night, over a hundred very satisfied customers served, and a self-proclaimed but generally acknowledged "Player King" in the city, perhaps even the state.

I live a life of "single servings". No hooks. No strings. My phone is full of booty-call contacts. In fact, I have a weekly roster of girls that if I'm any more pedantic about, I would make some kind of "chore" wheel.

That's me in a nutshell though: freewheeling and blissfully happy with my awesomely excellent bachelor life.

But I digress.

Or perhaps not, if I can segue back to what happened eight months ago. Since what happened with Marco and Nina was like the direct opposite of my whole entire life's endeavors thus far.

When I arrived at our usual bar, *The Irish*, the two of them were just stepping out.

I high-fived Marco as he went on his way out.

"See you later, man," he bid me.

Marco Welling was one of my closest friends from college and we hung out most nights with the same group of people since business school—for four, maybe five years by then.

On the other hand, Nina Simons was new. She had just moved to the city the month before. She was definitely gorgeous—tall, blonde, think Scarlet Johansson *before* she got her boobs reduced. But naturally, in deference to my friend, I never went there.

Though I did crane my neck to check out her ass as she walked out the door. Marco's arm was slung comfortably around her shoulders. I blew out a breath, shaking my head in respect.

"Hey Alex," Tyler Mitchell called out as I neared our usual booth.

I was going to nod in greeting at him but then I heard another sweet little "Hey Alex" from this redhead hottie at the bar, so...

Twenty-minutes later, I swung back around to our booth.

"Hey dude," I responded to Tyler, straightening out my

suit jacket and nodding to the rest of the group in greeting before sitting myself down in the empty seat beside Claire Hale. Tyler and Janice were sitting across from us.

Tyler had been Marco's best friend since high school and Janice Coleman, who used to be Tyler's long-time girlfriend, was now Janice Coleman-Mitchell, his wife of three years. Tyler and Janice were both entrepreneurs. They had started this "eco-friendly food wrap" business together a few years ago and somehow it had taken off. Claire was Janice's best friend and the group's resident lawyer. We'd all just been at that same bar celebrating a few weeks ago when she had made associate at her firm.

This was the group. Suffice it to say, I'd met the three of them through Marco.

"You just missed it," Janice told me as I poured myself one from the pitcher on the table.

"What?" I asked, not looking at her.

"Marco and Nina officially just got their exclusive on," Tyler informed me.

"And after only a month," Claire interjected.

"No!" I instantly exclaimed my disapproval. "What have I been telling him over and over? Monogamy is for dorks." I gestured my pint across the table. "You know, like you, Ty."

Claire snickered. Tyler just gave me a suffering look. And Janice made a face. "Thanks a lot, Alex," she quipped. "Coming from you, I'll take that as a compliment."

I was still a bit disturbed by the news. "Seriously? In this day and age?" My eyes distracted toward the bar where a flock of quite young hot things was converged.

Janice reached across the table and smacked the side

of my head. "That would be *under*-age to be specific," she pointed out.

I put up my hands in resignation. "Hey, hey, there's no harm in looking, is there? Back me up, Ty," I prompted.

Tyler's eyes darted up to me and then to Janice, looking flustered. "Whoa, hey." He put up his own hands. "I was absolutely *not* looking. Damn man, are you trying to get me in trouble?" he asked me, betraying his size with the look of fear in his eyes.

But the rest of us just laughed.

Tyler was like the most faithful guy ever. He had only ever had eyes for Janice. But it was always hilarious to poke fun at him about it. Especially hilarious for me since I couldn't imagine for a second being content with just the one girl, or having been in a relationship for as long as they've been.

Needless to say, I had never once looked at Janice that way. Although in my opinion, Tyler had lucked out. Janice was also pretty hot.

"Whatever, this seriously sucks." I smoothed my hair back. "I mean, Marco was my wingman. Who am I going to hit on chicks with now?" I went on to complain.

Claire gave me a withering look. "Oh please, since when did the great Alex Keaton need help hitting on chicks?" she mused. "This is the guy who has booty-calls on speed dial. The guy who needed only to walk into the bar earlier tonight before instantly managing to grab that unassuming redhead's attention—yes, we all saw you." She gave me a pointed nod, gesturing to the girl at the bar. "The guy who always says 'a handmade Italian suit picks up girls by itself'?"

I gave her an authoritative look. "If you do recall, as I've mentioned before, the most successful pick-ups involve two players: one to set up the game and the other to close the deal." I raised my eyebrows in a prompt. "Don't you remember, that time when Marco went to L.A. for two days, and we were at the bar—?"

"You mean last week?" Janice quirked her eyebrow, amused.

I ignored her and went on. "And my man Tyler here was too chicken to talk to these two hot Australian tourists with me? And what happened, Ty?"

"You went home with both of them," Tyler replied resignedly.

"That's absolutely right." I slammed my palm on the table. "I had to go home with *both* of them. Imagine if I only had some help." I paused facetiously. "Granted, by the end of the night, I didn't actually *need* any help, but—I'm a *sharer*. That's just the kind of guy I am."

Tyler laughed while both Claire and Janice shook their heads in derision.

"It's amazing. Just when I think I've heard the crassest thing come out of his mouth, he just keeps right on talking," Claire remarked to them and Janice laughed.

"It's not crass if it's true," I claimed with a sigh. "Anyway, Claire, can you please stop changing the subject? I know I am amazing but we're not talking about me right now, god," I feigned an embarrassed complaint and they all laughed again. "Tonight's surprise plot twist is about Marco and Nina." I reverted back to the topic at hand.

"So, was anyone surprised?" Tyler asked, looking at the rest of us once we'd all settled.

"I was." Janice put her hand up. "I'd always hoped that

Marco would get his head out of his ass and fix the biggest mistake of his life."

"Oh please, not that again." Claire groaned out loud, waving dismissively across the table as if the topic was a fly she could shoo away.

"Oh, that's right." I shot her a sideways look in recall. "You guys used to date. Like a billion years ago."

"Oh, come on, girl," Janice spoke up cattily. "Even if you weren't my best friend in the entire world, surely I would think that you have way more to offer than that dolt, Nina," she said, putting up her hands. "Granted, she's nice and all, but what about her is so winningly spectacular?"

"Probably her cup size," I muttered, not at all kidding.

That earned me a crude look from Janice. Tyler almost spurted out his drink. Claire laughed.

"Oh, come on." Janice sighed haggardly. "Surely, sophisticated guys such as yourselves—" She stopped short upon meeting Tyler's gaze, making a face before she focused her gaze on me. "Alex," she piped up expectantly. "Wouldn't you say that Claire here is just as hot as, if not more than say, those girls there at the bar?" She gestured toward the bar.

"Ew Janice!" Claire's eyes widened in horror. "Alex," she started to me with a firm warning tone. "I don't want you to even begin to answer that question."

Tyler and I laughed.

"Ohh." Janice shifted in her seat restlessly. "But this is so unfair!" She gave Tyler and me brief glances. "I need an impartial guy's opinion and all I have is this useless lump." She elbowed Tyler. "And Alex friggin' Keaton." She sighed again, sounding defeated.

"Janice," Claire started calmly. "Marco and I. That's ancient history. That was like—a million years ago."

"Try four."

Claire gave Janice's quip a narrow-eyed look. "Either way, nothing has changed since then. We're just friends now. We've moved on. So should you. This whole tangent is absolutely pointless." She threw up her hands.

"*Either* way," Tyler repeated loudly as if authoritatively. "Marco and Nina are our friends. If they want to enter into some form of disastrous, consequence-ridden, whirlwind, monogamous relationship, it's exclusively their problem, isn't it, babe?" he prompted Janice then.

"Exactly," Claire told Janice pointedly.

Janice rolled her eyes.

And I just shook my head, having gulped down my beer before getting up to stand. "And on that note, I'm going to go see if any of those girls—" I gestured back to the bar. "Or a combination of them—are willing to enter into some form of disastrous, consequence-ridden whirlwind with yours truly," I finished with a grin as I walked away.

When I came back to the table, Tyler and Janice had gone to get the next round. Claire was just sitting there, chipping off the beer bottle label with her thumb distractedly. She barely looked up when I sat back down across from her.

I narrowed my eyes. I should say I had a gift for sensing when women were particularly emotionally vulnerable, a talent which comes quite handy during the proverbial "happy hour". I could even say quite a few notches on my belt had been gained by being particularly sensitive to those sorts of vibes. Though I also had to say I'd never sensed them from Claire before.

"I volunteer," I spoke up, leaning forward.

"What?"

"I volunteer," I repeated.

"What are you talking about?" She gave me a strange look.

"To be your rebound guy." I shrugged with a presumptuous conceited grin. "I'd be happy to offer my services."

She gave me a distasteful look back. "Ugh, Alex!" she balked, aghast.

"What?"

"Thanks, but I'm not quite that desperate." She had an expression of revulsion in her eyes.

"Hey, I'm offended by that. What are you even talking about?" I chuckled airily, not at all offended. "Check this out," I coaxed, doing some exaggerated posturing in front of her.

She narrowed her eyes at me for a few seconds. "You are disgusting." And after a pause, she added, "And you still have that sleazy blonde's lipstick on your chin."

"Oh, oops." My eyes widened with only a half-embarrassed grin as I got a napkin from the table dispenser to wipe my chin and using the metal napkin dispenser as a mirror.

As it turned out, one of the hot blondes from the group of girls before had been more than eager to make out in the bathroom with the charming guy she'd just met. Maybe a little too eager.

Trust Claire to be neither too polite nor too shy to point it out. She always was the one with her head firmly on her shoulders. The no-nonsense no-B.S. arm of the group. The checks and balances.

In the past, I had always found that dull. That day, I was a little bit challenged.

I gave her a disarming smile, studying her clear blue eyes. "Just saying," I said, trying to sound conniving. "If you ever need to get back at that *jerk* Marco, I'll gladly toss you one."

But Claire just started to get up. "I gotta go. I'm gonna go say bye-bye to Tyler and Janice."

"Hey, come on." I stretched my arms across the backrest of the then-empty booth. "You're giving up a once-in-a-lifetime opportunity here," I called out as she walked away but she didn't even so much as glance backward. Though I craned my neck to check out her ass as she left—something I had honestly never thought to do before and I blinked, surprised —impressed. "Tsk." I shrugged again at the potential missed opportunity.

Aside from Janice, Claire was probably the only other female in the city that I wouldn't even have dreamed of hitting on. I had never once considered it because of the history with Marco, "bros before hoes" and all that.

But right then, I stopped to think. Since Marco had already moved on, perhaps it was also time for me to reconsider.

I mean, Claire was also pretty cute. And it seemed like a thing to do to pass the time.

Like, at least once anyway.

2

Marco and Nina Have a Party

A couple of weeks later, Marco and Nina had this party. I don't even remember what it was celebrating exactly. I just supposed that when people were happily "in love", or at least were still delusional in the "honeymoon phase", they always wanted to rub that happiness in other people's faces.

Fortunately for me, I was immune to that sort of stuff. I was there with a date—Miss Swipe Right #8.

The party was at Marco's parents' house. I'd always thought the house was designed specifically for having parties, with the open plan living, lounge, kitchen, customizable mood lighting, the awesome deck with the great view of the bay area, the giant-ass pool, and the poolside bar that had its own beer dispenser. I couldn't even begin to tell you how many awesome nights and parties have been had at that house.

That night was no exception.

I was getting some drink refills for me and my date (which was code for flirting with the hot female bartender) when Janice found me at the bar.

"Hey," I greeted over the noise of the party. "Tyler here yet?"

Janice yelled in my ear. "He's on his way," she said. "He's picking up Claire from some law school alumni event. Where's Candace?"

"Charmaine," I corrected.

"Oh, so you do bother to know their names?" Janice mused.

I had to laugh. "Why do you always underestimate me?" I asked her. "I can be a perfectly decent gentleman when I want to be."

She wiggled her eyebrows in agreement. "Yeah," she said wryly. "I can see that from your unnecessary large tipping at an open bar—oh, finally!" she exclaimed, starting to wave both hands as if to get someone's attention from across the way. "Ty!" she called out.

And when I glanced over, I had to blink myself out of a startle. Tyler was making his way up to the pool area where we were. But my eyes had snapped straight to Claire who was right behind him.

She looked jaw-dropping hot!

She was wearing a low-cut snug little white number and her light brown hair was down her shoulders, wavy and tousled.

"Damn girl, you lookin' fine tonight," Janice commented, giving Claire an appraising look as she and Tyler approached us.

Claire gave her a deadpan look before stealing her drink. "Is that alcohol? Great." And she chugged it down.

Janice's forehead creased. "Something wrong, sweetie?"

"No, no, just busy," Claire dismissed. "Some of the senior partners just decided to throw this case referral down the ranks and between that and dealing with the interns—"

I wasn't listening to the conversation but I was still staring at Claire. I would never have imagined that that body had been hiding under her usual three-piece business casual attire. Tyler had to elbow me to snap out of it.

He shot me a strange look. "Bro, you checkin' out Claire?"

"What? No," I replied quickly, instinctively, before I stopped short. "I mean, yes. Hell yes," I amended, figuring there was no shame in admitting it.

"She does look different tonight, doesn't she?" Tyler commented.

"Different," I echoed. That was an understatement.

"Have you seen Marco yet?" he asked me.

"Oh, uh." I blinked a few times to clear my head. "Not yet actually." I panned my gaze around the crowd and spotted Nina right away. She was wearing a shiny silver dress so it was easy to spot her. "There's Nina though. I bet if you stand close to her long enough, Marco will turn up," I remarked with a bit of sarcasm.

"Come on, Jan." Tyler took Janice's hand to pull her along in pursuit of Marco and/or Nina, leaving Claire standing beside me.

She didn't say anything. She wasn't even looking at me. But she took one of the glasses I was holding and drained it in seconds flat. I had to grin. "I see time away from Marco is agreeing with you," I commented, giving her look another once-over.

"Oh my god." Claire shot me an annoyed look. "Would you just shut up? I don't want to talk about it."

"Jeez, someone's having a really bad day," I noted passively then offered her the other glass of wine I had. "My offer still stands, you know," I said with another grin. "Whenever you want to get that palette cleansed."

Naturally, I had seen Claire's look of scorn before but it was particularly prickly tonight. "It's that fast, is it?" she cut in, before declaring. "Just because Marco's got a new girlfriend doesn't mean you're suddenly allowed to hit on me."

Just then, I noticed Claire's gaze distract somewhere and I looked up to see what it was.

Tyler and Janice had found Marco and Nina. Marco, inexplicably, was also wearing a shiny silver shirt for tonight's party.

I was about to snicker and remark something insulting about matching couple outfits to Claire but before I could say anything, Claire grabbed my second glass of wine, chugged that down then whirled around to walk away.

I tried to see where she went but she was instantly swallowed up by the party crowd.

Admittedly, I'd had a couple of drinks in me when I wandered into the house about an hour later. My date had gone to powder her nose and I was actually looking for the hot bartender whom I thought I had seen come into the house a few minutes earlier.

I easily recognized Claire through the ornate stained-glass door of one of the lounges on the ground floor. For sure, nobody else was wearing that dress tonight. The door was already ajar. It creaked slightly when I nudged it open.

"Hey Claire," I called out. "Do you need a drink refill?" I was being friendly. I mean, we were friends.

It was only a split second when she glanced back at me but I could tell right away what was going on.

Claire was crying.

I blinked in shock.

"Oh shit, Alex," she mumbled, clumsily wiping her face.

I shut the door after coming in. "Are you okay?" I asked, a little bit concerned.

She didn't reply. I heard her attempting to control her breathing from short gasps.

"Oh, jeez." I patted her back awkwardly. Obviously, I didn't know the first thing about comforting crying women. That was, without getting them to sleep with me.

I should have gone and looked for Janice so she could help Claire out. Instead, I asked, "Is this about Marco?" And I couldn't help to add, "I thought you said that was ancient history?"

I heard her take a long, deep breath. She still didn't say anything but the answer was plain. I'd had absolutely no idea that she had carried this torch for him for so long. It struck me as strange that even Janice didn't even seem to know how upset Claire was about this whole thing.

I watched her. Ironically, what was going through my mind was how talking about exes was specifically successful in making women feel vulnerable that they would feel the need to lean on your shoulder for support. And I actually knew exactly what I should do and say in these particular situations. But I hesitated for a moment. It was Claire, for god's sake.

But then finally, she spoke.

"He didn't even tell me..."

I tried to meet her gaze. "Well, maybe...he thought it would be better this way," I guessed, trying to be helpful.

"Oh god, what about this is better?" She sighed dejectedly.

I noticed tears stream down her face again and my frown deepened. "Sshh. It's okay. Come here," I shushed, pulling her toward me. It seemed natural to stroke her hair, have her face buried in my chest. At the same time, it felt clumsy and weird.

When Claire broke off sniffling for a moment to look up at me with those big, blue eyes, I just did what naturally came to me. I cupped her face in my hands and leaned down to brush my lips across her eyelids, just to soothe her, to make her stop crying. It just didn't seem right, her crying. I had never seen Claire like that before.

Then I realized my heart was pounding in my chest and instinctively, I leaned my head further down to taste her lips. I intended to be brief, light, comforting. But as soon as I felt her soft lips against mine, I kissed her again, more ardently the second time as though hungrily, my tongue parting her lips, tasting her tears.

Claire pulled away abruptly, bewildered at my actions.

I met her gaze, looking stunned myself.

Unfortunately, I knew exactly what she was thinking—the only thing she could have been thinking. My record with women was certainly nothing modest, and I knew that she knew full well it was absolutely within my capabilities to take advantage of her weak moment.

"Ugh, what the hell is wrong with you?" Claire broke off, sounding disgusted.

The stained-glass door rattled as it slammed closed behind her.

I blinked, trying to reconcile reality with what had just happened. *Whoa.*

I touched my mouth, blowing out a breath. I knew I definitely shouldn't have done that. That was a total mistake. But I paused in wonder and disbelief. That was one hell of a kiss. Claire was absolutely full of surprises tonight.

And I was suddenly revitalized. New mission: I totally had to hit that.

3

Marco and Nina Get a Cat

I wasn't sure what it was about couples but they tended to want to take care of things together. I would have thought like sharing a plant would have been the easy option but I supposed that wasn't enough of a responsibility.

That day when Marco and Nina decided to get a cat, I decided to tag along. Not that I was terribly interested in rescue animals. It's just that I knew Claire volunteered at the animal shelter.

Since the party at Marco's parent's house, I had taken on a new challenge.

I'd put a temporary hold on my weekly roster of hook-ups and one-night stands with a view to score what I considered the biggest, most ultimate hook-up ever. The surprisingly lovely Claire Hale would be the crowning glory of my year.

The mere accomplishment of it would be an incredible confidence boost and would surely carry my ego for months. But only if I managed to pull it off.

The plan was simple. I just had to always make sure to be around Claire every time Marco would be—at the bar, at parties, whatever. That way, if the time ever came again that she needed a shoulder to cry on, or perhaps more, I would be the first guy that she would see.

And I would be the most sensitive, most comforting, most decent gentleman in the world.

The perfect rebound.

Except it never seemed to work out.

Honestly, it was feeling like it had been a pretty long two weeks already. I guessed I had underestimated how long a mission like that would actually take, and what I would have to give up in the meantime.

I didn't even want to count the number of times I'd had to pass on hooking up already and how much sex I'd had since I started—way less. Not zero, of course, but I'd seriously had to cut down.

I knew it sounded completely cold but I also told myself that, to some degree, I was also going to be helping Claire get over Marco.

What better way to get over some guy than to do his super-hot best friend, right?

It was around Thanksgiving when we went to the animal shelter and the place was decorated for the holidays accordingly. Fake cardboard turkey on the counter, red and green paper cut-out chains hanging on the ceiling, certain volunteers wearing fake feathered headbands or pilgrim hats.

On the beat-up corkboard on the wall, under the heading: "Volunteer of the Month", I spotted a picture of Claire. She had put on a goofy expression on purpose. She had been volunteering at the shelter for years. It was one of those details about her that I'd never really paid attention to but had always known.

When Marco, Nina, and I came in through the doors, I immediately spotted Claire in the back.

She was playing with one of the dogs, waving a tattered little toy rabbit. Her hair was in a messy bun and her clothes had splotches of muddy water on them, but she looked so happy, her smile was bright and genuine. She was wearing an angel halo, instead of feathers.

Somehow, I thought it was appropriate. I couldn't help an involuntary smile.

Then Marco called out his greeting, "Hey, Claire."

Claire glanced up and her smile immediately faded upon seeing the three of us. Yup, probably the last three people she wanted to see.

Then Marco and Nina spent ten whole minutes describing to Claire the kind of cat they wanted to get. I had to stand there and listen to them jabber on, and in couple talk no less, like constant giggling and finishing each other's sentences.

A tabby, a kitten, a calico, something furry and cuddly, black with orange stripes—no, no, white with black stripes, or wait—black, white, and orange. They were going to share custody of the cat—half the week it would stay at Marco's, the other half at Nina's, but they wanted to make sure that the cat felt at home so that it didn't get too confused with the arrangement.

What the hell did it matter? It was a cat!

And after those ten whole minutes, when Claire led them through the gate in the back so they could have a look at the cats that were available, Nina glanced back at Claire, beaming mega-bright. "Thanks, Claire! You're a doll."

"Take your time. I'll be right here if you have any questions," Claire called melodiously, putting on her biggest and fakest smile.

I had stayed behind and had to laugh.

"What?" She darted a look back at me.

I pursed my lips, shaking my head as I leaned back against the counter. "You absolutely cannot stand to see them looking so happy, can you?" I prompted even though I already knew the answer.

Claire rolled her eyes and replied wanly, "I honestly don't give a flying rat's ass."

That made me chuckle again. Claire had always struck me as so prim and proper. Sure, I had heard her swear before but never as emphatic, or colorful.

She shot me another look as if to say 'what's so funny' but instead she asked, "What the hell are you doing here anyway?" as she purposelessly rearranged some flyers on the counter.

I stopped short, straightening up. "Oh, right."

I was on.

"Well, I..." I paused, pursing my lips again. "The truth is...I...actually wanted to apologize for—that time at Marco's party," I relayed, before clearing my throat. "I was totally out of line. Honestly, I was drunk. And I know it's been kind of weird between us since, so I just wanted to...clear the air."

It wasn't totally insincere, since ever since the last party,

Claire was being really careful not to be alone with me. And it wasn't always easy to make excuses as to why I was always around.

At the bar, sure. Out to dinner, or to the movies, no problem. But accidentally running into the three of them when Claire had accompanied Marco and Nina to the bank for some legal purpose, for example, did get a bit tricky.

To her credit, Claire was still always civil, always nice, although she would also always make a point never to linger.

Claire just looked at me with a blank look on her face and I swallowed hard, hoping she didn't see through the fake 80% of that apology. Turned out, I was in luck.

"Is that why you've been following me everywhere lately?" she finally prompted, peering at me with narrowed eyes. "You wanted to apologize?"

"Uh..." I hesitated then answered correctly. "Yes."

She blew out a breath, looking away. "Forget about it."

I watched her expression. It sounded as though I was instantly and completely forgiven, which was surprising since I knew a lawyer could quite just as easily argue that I should be arrested for assault.

I glanced over at Marco and Nina talking to one of the other animal handlers and then Claire asked the question I thought she would ask next.

"You didn't tell Marco, did you?"

I wondered if she was worried for a different reason like maybe she wanted to try to make him jealous. But I just shook my head, still carefully watching her face before I stated, rather than guessed, "And you haven't told Janice."

Because I knew if she had, a "storm" of Janice would have

definitely already come bearing down my head, and it was highly unlikely that I would have survived.

Claire gave me a look. "Are you kidding? Can you imagine if I told Janice any of this?"

I cracked a grin. We both knew Janice well enough to know the answer to that question.

Claire and I both watched the "happy couple" play with one of the kittens they picked up from the fenced-in little cat playing area. Claire didn't look sad or upset. But after a moment, I caught her take a deep breath in to sigh heavily.

I took a deep breath myself. "Ssso...who'd have thought, huh?" I gestured to Marco and Nina cooing over the cat.

She blinked up at me like she had only just remembered I was standing there before she shook her head, sounding rueful. "I'd just always thought Marco was a dog person," she said, shaking her head. "I guess I *really* was mistaken."

I furrowed my eyebrows at what I believed was misplaced remorse on her part. "Look," I started in earnest. "You could do so much better than Marco. Trust me." I shrugged casually. "I mean, you just have to pull out that hottie in the white dress again."

A corner of her mouth turned up, amused. "You liked that, huh?"

I looked away, chuckling again at her tenacity. She didn't even blush. "I mean, you know. That girl was smokin'!" I remarked. "Where've you been hiding that all these years?"

"Oh, you don't like this look then?" Claire quipped, gesturing to herself good-naturedly. "The 'just got peed on by dogs and got mud in her hair' look?"

"No, no." I laughed lightly. "This—this is good too," I

replied, nodding slowly, surveying her appearance. "But I mean, *that* girl—that girl could get any guy she wanted. I would kiss that girl again," I added offhandedly.

It didn't occur to me that Claire would get offended by my bringing that up again. But sometimes I say things I don't think through. It happens.

Her entire face clouded over and she shot me a poisonous look. "What the hell are you doing?"

"I'm just saying—I'm here for you, you know?"

Claire shook her head in loathing but not exactly disbelief. "You're such an ass."

Before I could say anything more, another girl came up to the counter just then. She was wearing a volunteer's pilgrim hat.

"Claire, sweetie, can you do the closing tomorrow? Pretty, pretty pleeease," she cooed at Claire, giving her the batty eyelashes treatment. "I have to take my mother's car to a mechanic and it's going to be such a drag if I have to keep driving her everywhere for another week."

Claire visibly groaned. "Seriously? Why am I always the one doing you favors? I closed for you twice already." She rolled her eyes before resigning anyway. "Fine, but this is the last time, okay? We all have other jobs too—and I don't mean just dancing at random clubs waiting to be discovered by Hollywood agents."

But the girl was looking up at me now. She gave me a cute little smile. "Hi."

I cleared my throat and smiled back at her. "Hi there," I said shortly.

Claire rolled her eyes again. "Daphne, Alex. Alex, Daphne," she recited mechanically.

Daphne giggled as she put out her hand to shake mine. "It's really nice to meet you."

"Likewise," I replied before looking back at Claire.

Claire had her eyebrows raised expectantly as she looked back and forth from Daphne and me since Daphne was still standing there.

I glanced back to meet Daphne's gaze again. She was still smiling up at me. I hid my groan and just turned back to her with, "Say, why don't you give me your number and I'll call you sometime?"

Daphne giggled again before she eagerly wrote her digits down on the back of one of the animal shelter business cards. "I get off at 6," she added. "Maybe I'll see you later?"

"Sure." I smiled back at her nonchalantly as I pocketed the business card.

When Daphne still didn't leave, Claire cleared her throat loudly and pointedly, "A-hem, don't you have some work left to do?" which made Daphne jump in surprise and only then finally walk away, but not without a glance back at me and another sweet smile.

I bit my lip in amusement, shaking my head as I turned to Claire to comment on the situation. But she put her hand up to stop me. "Don't even."

That was when Marco and Nina finally came back with a little gray kitten and Claire had to write them up some paperwork.

"Thanks for coming along, Alex." Nina beamed at me once it was all done. "Wasn't this so much fun?"

I had to stifle my laughter and was glad when Marco interrupted, except what he said next was, "We're going to get Chinese takeout for dinner. You two want to join us?"

Claire paled and I thought I saw the horror in her face at the thought of sharing a meal with the two lovebirds. It was the first visible reaction I had seen from her in response to the situation.

I decided to reply for her. "Raincheck, dude," I said as I mocked Marco a salute. "Claire said she was going to introduce me to this hot friend of hers who works here too—Daphne something."

Marco chuckled and he gave me a wink. "That's my man. No rest for the wicked, hey?" he remarked as he bid me a wave. Then he glanced up at Claire with a charming smile. "Thanks for the help, Claire. You're the best." And he and Nina left through the swinging double doors.

That last note made me involuntarily frown. Marco could really be so full of himself sometimes.

I turned back to Claire, expecting her to still be standing at the counter, perhaps recovering from the whole encounter, but she had walked over to the supply closet and when she came back, she had a broom, a mop, and a bucket on a little roller cart.

"I'll see you around, Alex." Claire gave me a brief nod as she opened the dog play area enclosure gate to let herself through.

I watched her for a moment, somewhat amazed at how she

had handled the entire thing, even with me hanging around and messing up the works.

Claire was totally unflappable. And I was stumped as to why on earth someone like her would be so hung up on Marco?

I mean, Marco was my friend. He was a great guy. But we were more alike than different. He was nearly just as shallow as I was. Before Nina, he also hit on girls at bars and lived the sweet, sweet bachelor life like myself. Neither of us read poetry or had any compelling political views.

What could Claire Hale possibly find so spectacularly winning about Marco "Ball is Life" Welling?

And for some reason, I felt an inexplicable impulse to know, to ask, or at least to stick around and discuss further how much I thought she and Marco were completely incompatible, but then—

"Alex, hi! You're still here." Daphne looked pleased as she came out from the back, fluffing up her hair. She walked straight toward me, taking my arm. "You're so sweet to wait for me."

Claire stopped sweeping and looked up.

I shot Claire a look of resignation, even though my grin had a tinge of arrogance.

Claire met my gaze wryly. "You know Alex, you're probably the only person who goes to an animal shelter and gets a date instead of a pet."

I grinned wider. "Seems to work."

"See ya later, Claire!" Daphne gave her a little wave.

"Daph," Claire piped up, giving her a meaningful look.

"Do you care at all that he's going to sleep with you and then never call you again?"

Daphne looked to be thinking about it as she twirled her auburn hair around her finger before she answered. "Not really... You can join us if you like," she offered.

I had to stifle my laughter even as Claire laughed out loud. "Whatever, guys. You absolutely belong together." She waved, more like waving us away instead of waving goodbye.

I met her gaze and Claire shook her head again in judgment. I could have been mistaken but I thought she also looked just a little bit impressed as well. I smiled. "Hey, seriously though," I called out with a nod as she rushed us toward the door. "I meant what I said before. That Marco's a dog. You deserve better."

Claire was still shaking her head in silent mirth and sheer disbelief. "I know!" she replied loudly, closing the door behind us.

I was still smiling to myself before I turned on my heel to walk away, slinging my arm around Daphne's shoulders.

4

Marco and Nina Move in Together

When Nina and Marco arrived at *The Irish*, Nina was already bubbling with joy as though she couldn't keep whatever it was in any longer. "We have *fantastic* news," she started.

I stopped in mid-drink to look up at them as Marco announced, "We're moving in together!"

For some reason, I instinctively glanced up in the direction of the bar where Claire was getting the next round.

Janice leaped out of her seat to give Nina and Marco hugs. "Congratulations, you guys!"

Tyler shook Marco's hand and he met Claire's gaze from behind him, giving her a big smile, as she arrived back. "Hey Claire, you just missed it—"

She shook her head quickly as she plunked down the

pitcher of beer on the table. "No, no, I heard it," she said as she sat down across the table from me.

"Well, that didn't take long, you lucky dog," Tyler was commenting to Marco, who had then turned to me for my reaction.

I raised my eyebrows at him. "Dude," I muttered, pretending to sound disparaging. I didn't want to rain on his parade but I couldn't exactly tell him that I thought for a second he was doing the right thing so I didn't say anything else.

But Marco just laughed as he put his arm around Nina once again.

I watched Claire from across the table as I could only imagine her irritation as the events unfolded, but from where I was sitting, it didn't show at all.

Through all the weeks of Marco and Nina's syrupy sweet couple banter at the bar, pet names, P.D.A., incredibly annoying couple posts on every form of social media available, and the whole nine yards that we'd all had to endure—through all of it—Claire had just been normal Claire, how she always was: zinging everyone with ironic quips, correcting the facts in Tyler's lame stories, joking around with Janice. Janice, who still seemed oblivious that Claire was probably dying inside every time she saw Marco reach out to brush Nina's hair out of her eyes—which was way too often.

Then again, Claire had absolutely no tells whatsoever. If I didn't know any better and hadn't personally seen her crying at that one party, I would believe there was absolutely nothing wrong too. And I figured that was also what Claire was intending for everyone to believe.

There were some moments though in the last couple of

weeks when Claire would happen to meet my gaze, and I would see a flicker of thought cross her mind, of despondency, of caution, of wariness. She knew I knew. And I was the only one who knew. But neither of us would speak about it.

It felt funny to be sharing a secret like this with Claire. At the same time, it felt somehow gratifying.

"Oh yeah, that sounds amazing," Claire's canned response to Nina's story about interior decorating sounded appropriately cheerful.

"We're going to have a cute little housewarming party this weekend, so you all better clear your schedules," Nina was relaying enthusiastically to Janice and Claire beside her. "We just need to get the place tidied up a little bit."

"This one has so many plans already." Marco gestured to Nina with a smile.

"I absolutely adore furniture shopping!" Nina gushed. "Marco and I have been looking around forever for a coffee table that would match the ambiance of our new lounge—"

I actually already had a date planned on the night when they were having their housewarming party but I knew I was going to ditch those plans instantly.

Claire was going to be at that party.

Besides—a housewarming party? Where all the chicks were frenzied with "nesting" hormones? I was so there.

****

Marco and Nina got a really "cute" apartment together. It was a two-bedroom loft, plus study, and it really was obvious which one of them was in charge of the interior decorating.

Nina had filled spaces with magazine-catalog types of furniture and accessory ensembles. Everything had flowers on it—the throw pillows, picture frames, table cloths, vases. And about half of their furniture was pink.

Though Marco didn't seem to mind, I noted on the night of the party. The guy was looking deliriously happy, holding a cheese platter as he chatted with some of the guests.

I was wondering how long their "honeymoon phase" would last, as I'd certainly seen my fair share of relationships that did not last. Case in point: my parents divorced. It seemed to be the new status quo.

But I was happy for my friend. Sure, I didn't agree with how he suddenly wanted to run his life, and I was still about half-and-half on whether or not he and Nina were actually going to last as a couple, but with Marco off the market, the good news was that I definitely had less competition. Claire notwithstanding.

Tyler and I were hanging around the much-talked-about new coffee table in the lounge. Janice and Claire had gone to the kitchen to get some appetizers.

I was looking critically at the glass tabletop. "I think I would have gone for something more natural. Something in wood with natural grains. I bet that would have looked really good with the skylight."

"Where's your date?" Tyler prompted me instead of responding to my comment as he surveyed the crowd around us.

I shrugged, taking a swig from my bottle. "Didn't bring one."

Tyler's eyebrows lifted in surprise. "That's been happening a lot, bro. What's going on?"

I pursed my lips in wordless reply.

"Don't tell me the great Alex Keaton is hard up on dates," Tyler teased good-naturedly.

I shot him an oh-please look.

The truth was that it was proving to be too much work to keep another girl engaged while I was on the look-out for another breakdown from Claire.

Like what had happened at the Christmas party when Marco and Nina arrived and I thought Claire was going to walk out in a fit, but she had only gone outside the venue to take a phone call.

Yeah, my date hadn't appreciated having been left in the middle of the dance floor all of a sudden. So that was an easy lesson learned.

Quite frankly, it was getting irritating. This whole thing with Claire was seriously getting in the way of the babes front. It had been over a month and I was still getting nowhere. If anything, I even felt as though I was just actually making my chances worse. And did I mention—already down to twice a week!

Any other self-respecting guy would have given up weeks ago. But I told myself that for the purposes of my lofty mission, certain sacrifices were necessary. Good things came to those who waited. And I reminded myself that immediately after Claire, there would surely be no lack of babes willing to crawl back all over me as much as I wanted.

"Ty, look around." I gestured to the room. "This party is crawling with available chicks. And thanks to Nina, there's a fresh new batch of girl-friends in attendance who may otherwise not have had the opportunity to meet my awesome self."

Tyler just chuckled before he tapped my arm. "You haven't said much lately about Marco and Nina's nosedive into deeply committed relationships. Do you finally approve or just shutting up to be nice?"

"Pass," I replied nonchalantly.

"What's the matter? You don't think they suit each other?" Tyler prompted.

I made another big show of shrugging. "I don't know," I said flippantly. "Is that all it takes? If you ask me, inviting some girl to share all your stuff is like inviting a lawsuit waiting to happen. I don't know," I repeated. "Eventually, you gotta think about her feelings, and *your* feelings, and her priorities, and *your* priorities. Do I like pink furniture? Should I say something? Why *does* she take forever in the bathroom? Does she really wish I made more money or was she just kidding? Maybe she really does look fat in those jeans. Maybe I don't want to meet her parents. Are we moving too fast? Are we moving too slow? Then it gets even *more* complicated. Certainly too complicated for me," I concluded with another shrug.

Tyler laughed out loud. "I love how you've boiled commitment down to a thirty-second rant."

"Hey, if the shoe fits," I mumbled, taking another sip of my drink.

"Huh," Tyler huffed. "All I know is when I met Janice, everything in my life just fell into place, you know? It seemed like the simplest thing in the world. It sort of felt like the cruisy bit you get to near the end of a race."

"Well, you never did like the race," I pointed out, shaking

my head. "Janice was right. You are a useless lump. You make it all look too easy," I said just as the girls came back.

"Who's easy?" Janice wanted to know, looking curious, overhearing the end of my sentence.

Tyler jerked his thumb in my direction. "Alex thinks our relationship is too easy."

And Janice laughed. "Oh Alex, my poor uninformed single friend," she began. "No relationship is easy," she declared. "Some can be simpler than others, but they all need work. If you ask me, the problem nowadays is that people just give up too fast. I think...when you love someone, you don't just give up. You do the work."

"What about when things just aren't meant to be?" Claire put in, her tone sounding very neutral as she munched on some mozzarella sticks. "No matter how hard you work. It can happen."

I shot her a quick look. She absolutely sounded like she was making a general observation or commentary on the nature of human relationships or the world, but these days I was never sure if there was any deeper meaning or personal weight to the things that Claire says.

"Well, I suppose there's that too," Janice conceded. "I guess all I'm thinking is it takes a certain level of maturity to be able to commit to another person. And I think it's very mature of Marco to be taking this step with Nina," she said. "I'm glad to see the rest of us are growing up," she quipped, giving Claire a meaningful glance.

Claire shot her a skeptical look. "Uh, I think you better check your aim. I'm not the one here exclusively predisposed to having meaningless hook-ups." She tilted her head pointedly in my direction. "In fact, I think Alex's last big commitment was to this hairstyle."

Tyler and Janice laughed.

I shot Claire a look, taken aback, but then put my hands up defensively. "Hey, hey, I'll grow up when I'm good and ready," I told them all airily before smoothing my hair back. "Also, you don't change a classic look when it's always working for you."

Claire bit her lip to keep from laughing and I gave her a brief questioning look. I couldn't believe she was trying to provoke me when she knew full well I could expose her big secret right then and there.

But she must have just realized it herself as she then proceeded to immediately steer Tyler and Janice away from me.

"In any case, I think we'd better let Alex's hair get back to work. Heaven forbid he miss out on the next opportunity to whore himself out. Come on, guys." She beckoned and the three of them walked away, leaving me with a look of pure astonishment and disbelief.

I glanced up at Claire. She was standing with Tyler and Janice in a little social sub-circle, drinking and mingling with the other party guests.

I was across the room, occupied with hitting on Tessa, this model/actress that I had subsequently run into. Since after that putdown from Claire, I needed a little ego rub. Besides, it wasn't like I had anything else to do.

"Yeah, my job can be really challenging work but it *is* very rewarding. One of the best perks is that I basically make my own hours, so I'd be happy to check out some bodegas with you sometime," I was telling her.

I was being "Mr. Helpful Guy" since I had learned that Tessa had also just moved into town. I had impressed her with my expertise on all the cool spots in town, pretending to be knowledgeable about the best restaurants and dry cleaners. It was right around when I started talking about my Jaguar when she got really impressed and we snuck off to one corner so she could impress me with her own talents.

Right then, I heard Marco and Nina step out of the kitchen with food refills, announcing something about some kind of organic gluten-free bean dip before proceeding to relay stories about their new Keto diet and how they've both been sharing their work-outs with each other, the two of them looking perky and happy.

I stopped in mid-make-out to peek around Tessa's head and look toward the main room where my friends were.

"Alex, what are you doing?" Tessa was not at all happy to be paused.

"Just a second," I mumbled, craning my neck to watch Claire for a moment.

But just as she had been doing for the last few weeks or so, every time she saw Marco, she would just get a blank look on her face, take a deep breath, paste a smile on her face, and then immediately go back to party business.

I pursed my lips in slight irritation, my enthusiasm for resuming "formalities" with my actress dampening. But I just gave Tessa's prompting gaze a wan smile before I leaned back into it.

Fortunately, she was keen to continue. Admittedly, sometimes it didn't turn out that way anymore.

A little while later, Tessa and I had decided to whisk ourselves back to my place for...an extended guided tour of the city and I was getting our coats by the door, waiting for her to come back from the ladies' room when just then, I spotted Claire hurriedly going up the stairs. And she looked a bit upset.

I straightened up in alert.

I was on.

Could this be the night?

I left the coats and hastened upstairs, following suit.

Claire was in the second room I poked my head into, what looked like a potential guest bedroom. She was sitting on the bare mattress, staring into space.

She looked startled when she noticed me by the doorway. "Oh god, Alex, why are you here?" Irritation was clear in her tone.

"I was just..." I tried to make an excuse but came up at a loss.

"I just want to be alone, okay?" Claire told me, her forehead still creased.

I hesitated for a moment before decidedly stepping through the door. "Um, what's the matter?" I asked, walking closer.

She shot me an annoyed look. "Nothing I want to talk to *you* about."

"Okay, should I...get Janice then?" I offered, moving to get my phone.

"No," Claire cut in almost immediately and I met her

gaze in understanding. She *still* hadn't told Janice about any of this yet.

"Claire." I shrugged pointedly. "I mean, you look like you need to get something off your chest."

She shook her head as though in disbelief. "Nothing. It's completely ridiculous. You wouldn't understand. Would you please go away?"

"Oh come on," I coaxed. "Are you seriously going to keep all that inside just because you're too stubborn to talk about it with someone like me?" I gave her a meaningful look. "I know I'm not the world's most sensitive guy but who else can you talk to about this?"

She pursed her lips, looking frustrated that my argument had some semblance of logic in it, and looking more annoyed that I was right, before she relayed, "I just saw—Nina's diplomas."

I raised my eyebrows. "Her...diplomas?" I echoed, thinking I heard her wrong.

"Yes, diplomas. Plural," Claire said as though she couldn't believe it. "They were framed and hanging in the study downstairs, and *apparently*—" She paused, tossing her hair emphatically. "Nina Simons has a bachelor's degree from business school *and* a master's degree in business management. And not from some two-bit community college either."

My forehead was still wrinkled as I couldn't understand how that would make her so upset but then she stood up, threw her hands up in the air, and began to pace as she explained at length.

"Nina Simons—is smart!" Claire exclaimed. "That blonde dolt is not a blonde dolt at all! I had always thought the reason that Marco and I didn't work out was because he wanted someone less intellectual. I had always thought that it was the main thing that he couldn't deal with about me. But dammit!" She sighed heavily, disparagingly. "If he was just going to end up with a smarty anyway, then why wasn't it me?"

I narrowed my eyes at her, pausing, sort of in astonishment before I started, "What the hell are you talking about?" I met her gaze. "Nina Simons has got nothing on you," I told her, bracing my hands on her shoulders. "Does she have a license to practice law in three countries? Does she do volunteer work? Did she shake hands with the Dalai Lama at the Charitable Trust event last year? When was the last time Nina got asked to assist with translations at the UN? Did *she* just make associate at her big fancy law firm? Does she consistently beat everyone else on *every kind of movie trivia game* known to man?" I prompted emphatically, my eyebrows raised. "Plus...you don't know that that diploma wasn't fake. She could have just printed that out," I reasoned lamely.

At that, at least, Claire shot me a look of ridicule.

I chuckled a little. "Look," I started seriously, pulling her back to sit down on the edge of the bed in front of me. "You said it yourself, you were all wrong about Marco. Are you really crying in a room about that guy who likes cats? Really? That guy?"

"No. No." She shook her head again, as though collecting her wits. "I was right. The Marco that I thought I was going out with wasn't even real at all. I imagined him. He was just this guy that I kind of liked, and then I built up the rest of his personality in my head and only saw what I wanted to see."

I blinked again, a bit bemused by the depth of her analysis.

"Great—listen, how about we get out of here?" I proposed with a disarming smile. "I think I saw a Starbucks around the corner. We can talk it all out and—"

Claire cut me off, rolling her eyes automatically. "God's sake, Alex, are you trying to hit on me again?"

"What?" My eyes widened. "No."

She gave me an oh-please look.

"No, seriously," I said firmly, putting up my hands in resignation. "Just coffee." I paused for a second. "And...if we happen to have sex afterward well, then that's just a bonus," I added airily.

"Yeah, maybe for you," Claire concluded flatly, starting to get up.

"Oh come on, it'll be great," I vowed, resisting the faint urge to be actually offended.

Did she just forget whom she was talking to? It wasn't like every other girl I'd been with didn't sing me enough praises. I basically had it on good authority that I was the best ever lay in the entire bay area.

"Goodbye, Alex." Claire brushed past me brusquely on her way toward the door.

"Claire, Claire, Claire, come on." I caught her shoulder lightly before she could leave. "Give me one good reason why not," I prompted, giving her a challenging look.

I had never had to work so hard to get a girl into bed before. My heart was pounding in my chest, in anxiety, in anticipation.

Claire stopped short, unfazed. She gave me an even look before she started. "Alex, your life is a train wreck waiting to happen," she said emphatically. "I actually feel sorry for you, and all of those girls who don't know any better than to fall for—" She gestured at me. "All this. Your charming smile and empty promises. And I sure as shit don't want to be around when you finally run out of steam and realize your whole entire life had been a meaningless quest, from one shag to the next."

My jaw dropped. *Ouch.*

Claire blinked, her mouth slightly open, as though she knew she had said too much. But without another word, she whirled around and walked out the door.

5

⸎

Marco and Nina's New Year's Eve

I guessed New Year's Eve parties were important for couples. New Year's has that "brand new" feeling that they just can't resist having to share with that someone they love, kissing at midnight, fireworks, and the usual fuss about starting the year over as if it was all that important.

We went to a party at the Palace of Fine Arts near the waterfront. The five of us arrived at the big party in a fancy-ass limousine. The limo had been Marco's idea—something to make the night more special, or something or other. Claire was going to meet us at the party later on because she had some other lawyer-y event to attend first.

In spite of myself, I was really looking forward to seeing Claire at the party.

For one, I had convinced myself that what had happened

at Marco and Nina's housewarming party was just a minor setback. That if anything, I was wearing her down. And for another, thanks to my mission, it had become sort of automatic for me that every time I arrived at a party, I would have to immediately look for Claire. Like an impulse, almost an instinct.

"Wow, this is beautiful," Nina breathed as we stepped out to the party.

The Palace of Fine Arts was decked to the nines with twinkly lights and adding the disco laser lights and fake fog made the party and the night look absolutely mysterious and exciting.

Like anything could happen that night.

I spotted the countdown being projected onto a large screen across the lagoon. It was about two hours before midnight.

Marco and Nina immediately headed for the dance floor. Tyler and Janice immediately went for the buffet. I followed Tyler and Janice closer to the drinks area.

Right at that moment, and for the first time ever, I felt like a fifth wheel.

But I stayed by the bar, nursing my gin and tonic, resisting the urge to hit on the (again) female bartender, and visually assessing the rest of the party in case there was somewhere better I should be parked.

The night was a bit crisp but I could see it didn't stop some girls from wearing bare-all dresses.

I stopped short, grinning as I was reminded that neither Tyler nor Marco had the freedom to hit on any of these totally hot party girls.

Ah, the perks of being the fifth wheel...

Claire arrived at the party about a half-hour later. She had come in right when a new burst of fake fog covered the steps, almost as if it was on cue. Her entrance was almost magical.

And as soon as my gaze landed on her, my pulse began to race nervously, excitedly. And since I knew she would be making a beeline for them, I actually had to step away from Tyler and Janice to pull myself together first.

It was very uncharacteristic. And unsettling as hell. It didn't matter that she was just wearing a pretty sensible long black strapless dress. Though I did notice quite a few other guys had also turned to look when Claire walked in.

And who could blame them? She was absolutely stunning.

I shook my head briskly to snap out of it.

This was absolutely ridiculous. To me, girls were a dime a dozen. Not one of them should elicit this type of response or reaction. It was all the fake fog's fault.

So I decided right then that there was no point abandoning tradition.

I ditched Tyler and Janice before Claire could walk up to us.

It was Alex Keaton's New Year's Eve. I was going to get back out into the party crowd, enjoy myself as per usual, and hook up with the hottest girl and/or girls I could find.

Surely, my little quest could wait one night.

Unfortunately, Marco had other plans.

Right around T minus ten minutes to midnight, the night delivered on the unexpected happening.

I was about to close the deal on this really cute art school grad student when I noticed everyone on the dance floor suddenly stop moving all at the same time and make way for this couple—and when I looked over, what I saw bowled me over so much, I seriously almost choked on my drink.

Marco was proposing to Nina.

He was literally down on one knee with an open ring box in his hand. In the middle of the party. In the middle of the dance floor. Like slap bang in front of the lagoon.

It took a full second to register the implications of the event in my head and I held my breath, my eyes widening instantly, and for the next few minutes, I frantically tried to search the masses and masses of the party crowd in the foggy darkness to spot Claire. I hadn't been keeping tabs on her for a change so it was not only difficult, it was damn near impossible!

Of all the goddamn nights not to keep track of her!

But she found me first.

Claire grabbed my tux jacket and pulled me after her toward the back area. And before I even realized what was going on, she had pulled my head down and her lips had found mine.

Her kiss was hot, demanding. I could barely believe it. But I shifted gears easily and began to kiss her back just as passionately, backing her up against one of the columns, bracing her hands on her either side.

***

You know sometimes when you anticipate something so much, you think, when it finally happened, it couldn't possibly be as good as you've built it up in your head?

Oh, it was. It was so much better.

I collapsed on my back against the bed breathlessly, my mind still whirling.

I couldn't believe what had just happened. More to the point, I couldn't believe how good it felt.

I narrowed my eyes, somewhat bewildered, still trying to catch my breath. I was still shaking and every inch of me was still tingling. I almost thought I was going to black out for a moment.

Claire, however, sat up in bed, clutching the sheets to her chest, though she too was still heaving lightly.

The smile came to my face involuntarily. I reached out my hand to stroke her bare back, sitting up myself to plant a soft kiss on her shoulder. "That—was absolutely amazing," I said in a low husky whisper.

But when she glanced over and met my gaze, the expression in her eyes made me frown. She didn't look happy at all, or comforted, or satisfied.

She visibly swallowed hard, taking a deep breath and looking away, before speaking, "I shouldn't have done that. Oh god, what have I done?"

My frown deepened but I couldn't quite fully grasp why. "What's wrong?" I asked, looking concerned.

She wouldn't meet my gaze again. "I've just had sex with Alex Keaton," she stated, sounding in shock. "I have become a notch on Alex Keaton's bedpost. Oh my god, what is wrong with me?"

My chest constricted at her words. She made it sound so contemptible. I, on the other hand, couldn't even begin to imagine regretting any second of it. In fact, strangely enough, I wanted more.

"There is absolutely nothing wrong with you," I tried to reply in earnest. "You are passionate and sexy, and so goddamn beautiful. And you're a *wildcat* in bed," I said with a slight grin. My chest felt full. It was as though I could feel her mere presence enveloping me.

But when she spoke again, her voice broke. "He's engaged."

There was a lump in my throat. She was still thinking of Marco. I raised my hand hesitantly to touch her again. I stroked her hair. "He...has no idea what he's missing," I told her.

She hastily wiped her face with the back of her hand and vaulted up off the bed, putting on clothes in a hurry. "I have to get out of here," was all she said, and after all but two minutes, she bolted out the door, slamming it shut.

My heart pounded in my chest again.

It finally happened! Mission accomplished! I had finally done it. Congrats to me!

It was supposed to be time to change the sheets, have a shower, put on another suit, and head out to find the next conquest.

Instead, I sat up in bed, my eyes pinned to the door.

***

At *The Irish* the next day, there was quite a bit of festivity. Most of it a New Year's day party. And then, of course, there was the celebration for the brand spanking new happy news.

Marco and Nina were engaged.

I walked through the door just in time to catch the tail end of Tyler's congratulatory speech at our usual booth.

"—we're really happy for you guys," Tyler said, raising his glass.

"Cheers," Janice chimed in brightly, clinking glasses with Claire, Marco, and Nina.

Marco and Nina giggled happily as they kissed just as I arrived.

"Whoa, hey," I called out. "Stop that you two. What are you, engaged or something?" I joked.

"Dude!" Marco pulled away from Nina to come up and give me a brotherly hug.

"Congrats, bro." I patted his back before glancing over at Nina. "You're a lucky guy having locked that down," I remarked with a teasing tone.

"Oh Alex," Nina said, looking embarrassed, though I couldn't tell if it was pretend or not.

"Hey, guys." I gave my cursory nod at Tyler and Janice, but the moment I turned to look at Claire, she looked away. I guessed I should have expected that.

The truth was that I didn't know what to say to her. It actually served me right for being too impulsive, too focused on the goal. I'd never once even considered the fallout.

Obviously, I'd never had to hang out the next day and pretend to be just friends with any of the other girls I'd hooked up with. I had never spent the rest of the previous night racked with guilt and anxiety and anticipation either. It was very disconcerting.

It was actually a relief that everyone was preoccupied with discussing the engagement and the upcoming wedding.

Oh jeez, Marco was getting married. That just sunk in.

"I absolutely love my ring," Nina gushed to Janice and Claire. "Don't you just love it?" She displayed her hand in front of their faces. "Marco picked it out himself. He probably knew I'd just love it."

"Nina wants a June wedding, of course," Marco was telling Tyler. "I was thinking maybe Vegas."

"We know six months seems too soon—" Nina was going on and on.

"Noo," Claire interjected as though in ridicule.

Nina giggled again, bubbly and light. "You're right! Nothing's too soon with true love," she said, leaning back against Marco, who put his arm around her waist.

"Bro, I just thought of the best bachelor party to throw for you," Tyler told Marco.

I decided to cut in. "Hey, if anyone's planning the bachelor party, it is the only bachelor actually left in this group," I pointed out.

Marco laughed. "Just make it great, alright?" he directed. "And I don't want any of that low-key shit that Tyler wanted."

That made me laugh and I patted Tyler's back in consolation. "Dude, leave it to me," I told Marco. "I'll make sure to give you a very high-key night."

"Yeah, exactly! From now on, I want everything to be...legendary," Marco declared.

Tyler shook his head. "Marco, man, you're setting a dangerous precedent for your married life. I mean, how are you ever going to top that proposal?" he asked before gulping down his drink.

"Yeah, and anyway, how did you manage to plan that big

fancy proposal without Ty or me knowing about it?" I wanted to know.

"Some guys from work helped me. Seriously, you two are shit at keeping secrets," Marco told us.

Tyler laughed. I didn't. I cast a brief glance over at Claire again but she seemed highly concentrated on what Nina was saying.

Nina had her phone out and was showing everyone like two hundred pictures from last night's proposal. "I thought it was absolutely perfect," she breathed dreamily. "It was the absolute perfect way to kick off our New Year's together. I tried looking for you all afterward for a toast but the party was absolutely crazy! Like, Ty and Janice were there at the bar. But I couldn't find you, Claire. And you were gone too, Alex." She glanced up at me, touching my arm briefly.

"Yeah, where did you guys go anyway? We didn't see you after the midnight countdown," Janice asked, though she sounded less than curious as she refilled her drink from the bottle.

I shot Claire another quick look but she was pretending to be checking her phone. "I uh…I hooked up with a girl, of course," I replied nonchalantly, in a manner so as not to invite any further questions, with a 'nothing to see here' shrug.

"Claire—," Janice began.

"I'm busy." Claire waved abruptly, seriously committing to her checking-the-phone bit.

"Fine, she doesn't care," Janice drawled before turning to me. "Ty and I met this guy we thought Claire should hook up with last night," she relayed. "He's an architect."

I pursed my lips, unsure how I was supposed to react. "Mm-hmm, that sounds interesting," was all I said.

An architect. That sounded stable, and responsible, and mature. I frowned. He was probably also the nicest guy in the world. I didn't want to listen to the rest of the story but Marco and Nina were making out across the table so I obviously had to look the other way.

"Claire—Claire, did you hear me?" Janice whacked Claire's arm, making her begrudgingly put down her phone. "An architect," she repeated, nodding in a prompt.

"Janice," Claire groaned. "You know I hate being set up. And frankly, I don't think I really trust your judgment."

"Oh, come on, I found Ty well enough on my own, didn't I?" Janice said stubbornly though good-naturedly. "And he's a perfectly decent guy. What could it hurt? It's not like you're seeing anyone right now. How long *has* it been anyway since your last date?" Her forehead creased as if straining to actually remember.

I saw Claire take a deep breath, her façade beginning to show cracks.

Knowing what I knew, I was actually amazed at how much of this dribble Claire could put up with. I would have thought that Nina's onslaught of gush would already have been too much for Claire. But amazingly enough, it still wasn't.

"Look, blind dates are almost as bad as internet dating. They're for old maids and suckers. They're just not my thing," Claire rationalized. "So, thanks but no thanks."

"We're not saying you're any of those things, Claire," Tyler put in. "We just think it's not a bad way to meet new people either."

"But you won't even know each other, and you're obliged to be too polite, you never know where you stand—no, no." Claire shook her head firmly. "Hard pass."

"But he could be just the guy you've been looking for!" Janice insisted. "And if he's not—" She shrugged. "Then maybe you just do it Alex-style, you know? Go big the one night?" she quipped with a grin.

I blinked, surprised at the reference, and when I looked up at Claire automatically, she finally met my gaze.

"Come on, Alex," Janice coaxed me. "Tell Claire she deserves some fun too."

And that did it.

Claire stood up, excusing herself from the group with an intentionally vague "And that's my limit. I'll see you guys later, okay?"

I stood up almost instantly to follow her to the door. I knew I had to get her alone.

I was attempting to mask my nerves with a big grin but she knew full well I was behind her.

Before I could say anything at all, she whirled around to face me to firmly say, "Please. I don't want to remember. Can we just forget it ever happened?"

I stopped, suddenly at a loss. "I..." I could barely breathe. Forget? I barely slept last night thinking about it.

"I hope you haven't told anyone yet." She looked distraught like she couldn't stand the mere thought that I had already seen her naked. "I don't want..." She stopped short, taking a deep breath. "I just can't be one of those girls, Alex."

I shook my head slowly. "N-no. I haven't told anyone."

There was no mistaking the wave of relief coming over

her expression. "Thank you for that," she said. "I'm going to go now, but...I think it would be best if we don't hang out together for a while."

I frowned. "What? Are you—are you saying we can't be friends anymore?"

She gave me a plain look. "We were never really friends, Alex. You just happen to hang around *my* friends a lot. So maybe...you could hang out with your other friends for a while? Please?" she stated before turning around and disappearing amongst the sidewalk crowd.

I felt as though I got punched in the face.

Happy New Year, Alex.

Okay, so this story is about me a little. But none of this would have happened if stupid Marco and Nina hadn't decided to get married.

6

Marco and Nina's Engagement Party

I didn't go.

I'd made some lame excuse about work so that Marco wouldn't bust my ass about not attending his fancy engagement party.

Of course, I had to swear under the pain of death to show up at the actual wedding in return for flaking out at the engagement party. In any case, I knew I had to. I was a groomsman after all.

But I'd had the ultimatum from Claire and I didn't want to be a jerk. That was, an even bigger jerk than she already thought I was.

This time, my mission was reversed. I was in no way about to attend any party if I knew that Claire would be attending, or be around anywhere that I knew she would be present.

Naturally, this meant that I had missed every other party since New Year's. And I hadn't been hanging out at *The Irish* either.

I still went out for the rare beer with Tyler and Marco, but elsewhere, and only when I was 100% sure the girls would not be showing up.

And whenever Tyler would ask me where I had been, my standard response was only "Nowhere. I just needed a new scene."

I didn't feel like reactivating my hook-up chore wheel or exploiting Tinder again yet.

Don't get me wrong, I still went out and about town and had the usual one-night stand when the opportunity presented itself. It wasn't like the city had run out of available babes, however much they all paled in comparison to Claire.

I hung out with my other friend Rob quite a bit. We went to the same gym. He was also single, except he was a few years older, already been divorced once, really jaded, and everything that came with that particular set of circumstances.

His motto was "Screw the past. And screw tomorrow. Screw today. Screw everything."

I mean, we spent Valentine's Day at a strip club.

"She's a skank," Rob hollered after his last lap dance had left.

I just shook my head, amused as I took a sip of my scotch.

"Hey, what about you, man?" Rob gestured at me. "You've only had one all night. What, you don't like the girls here? I mean, yeah, I didn't realize how skanky they all are. Maybe Tuesday's girls were just better. I was only here once before on a Tuesday. I'm usually at '*The Leopard Skin*'. Now you really wanna have some fun, come to the *Leopard* on a Monday night," he advised with a grin.

Admittedly, hanging out with Rob was definitely not the most intellectually stimulating or morally encouraging pastime. Rob was almost a fine example of every bachelor's dystopian future. I supposed if I was going to look at the bright side, I could think that at least I hadn't ended up like Rob yet.

"Hey, if you're strapped for cash right now, I can spot you another lap dance," he offered, already raising his hand to call someone.

"Oh, no, no, I'm good. It's not that," I assured him with a nod so that he dropped his hand. "This is fine." I gestured to the pole show.

I guessed I'd never realized how much my social life had become dependent on "the gang."

Tyler and Janice always had some friends who threw parties for random reasons. Marco's parent's house was almost always lit up for some special occasion. Without the group, I had to rely on my visiting the random clubs and bars to find girls.

Not very many opportunities to "whore myself out" as Claire had put it, I remembered with a frown, trying not to think of the irony.

I didn't know why I couldn't stop thinking about Claire.

I had known Claire for years. But suddenly, everything I knew about her was all at once coming back to me.

Every darn little ridiculous adorable thing.

The way she wrinkled her nose, pretending to be repulsed when she's actually amused. Or that look she'd give you right before she just knows you're about to be schooled. The way she tried not to laugh at lame jokes, the infectious sound of her laughter when she just couldn't help it.

Contrary to her often sarcastic, highly logical front, I knew she was a total sucker for sappy sentimental ads on TV. She was the only one who would still bother to have pointless mundane debates with me, usually regarding the existence of mythical things, loch ness, aliens, that kind of stuff.

She had given me this non-fiction Carl Sagan book about space for one of my birthdays. I'd never read it. I told her so the year after. That was the last time she ever gave me a book.

I suddenly felt like I wanted to be that guy. The guy she had thought that I was. The kind of guy that would read that book. The kind of guy she would agree to get coffee with without making a face like it was the most horrendous thing she could ever think of. The kind of guy you would still want to spend the rest of the next day with, after having a night of the most mind-blowing sex with him.

Everything about her was confusing me like hell. I wanted to put her out of my mind. Not to mention what had happened with Claire had seriously shaken my confidence. I'd never felt so inadequate before in my entire life.

I went out with this girl last night. She was great. She'd said I was great too. But right after the "festivities", she'd gotten dressed right back up and was out the door after ten minutes. Sure, she was legitimately a flight attendant on a layover with an early flight two hours thereafter. But it still shook me.

"Are you still recovering from last night—what was her name? Natalia?" Rob prompted me as he popped some Swedish meatballs in his mouth.

"Natasha," I corrected. "No, it was fine."

"Fine?" Rob echoed. "Just fine?" He wrinkled his forehead. "Whoa, dude, don't tell me you're having some kind of—" He whistled suggestively before adding, "guy problem—down there."

I shot him a look. "What?" I asked, quickly dismissing it. "Don't be ridiculous. I am 100% fully operational *down there*."

"Well, that's a relief." Rob blew out a breath. "I've been sitting here with you all night and that is not the kind of infectious problem I need at this point in my life."

I shook my head, chuckling. "You can put your mind at ease then," I advised. "I just—" I hesitated before relaying, "I just can't stop thinking about this girl I slept with last month. Now *she* was a total firecracker in the sack. I mean, to say *I* was impressed is saying enough to her credit."

"Ooh, does she live on Nob Hill? Is her name Tiffany? I've met her," Rob volunteered, gulping down his drink.

"No...no." I tried to recall. "I don't think you've met her."

"Damn, maybe I should if she's so hot even *you* can't stop thinking about it," he remarked.

I frowned, having obviously no intention to make those introductions. "Nah, forget it. It's nothing," I dismissed nonchalantly.

"Is that why you're hanging out with me so much lately? Something happen with this girl?" Rob asked, grabbing a handful of nachos from the table.

I pursed my lips, trying to think of a different excuse. "No, that's not it. My uh—friend is getting married later in the year," I replied, only half-fibbing before making a show of shrugging. "And I just can't deal with being around him for the moment."

"Aha!" Rob gave a shout of laughter. "And another one bites the dust!"

I cracked a grin, nodding.

Since his divorce, Rob had become quite predictable, and I supposed one of the things we had in common was that we had the same incontrovertible opinion regarding marriage and commitment.

"Right? And he's only known the girl what—six months?" I said, somewhat in ridicule. "They're claiming it's true love."

"Bull-crap!" Rob exclaimed. "I had known Amanda two whole years and I still never found out she was a vapid whore until way at the end."

"You should see this girl though," I remarked, shaking my head as I thought of how to describe Nina in the fewest words. "She's like...total eye-candy if the candy was the entire Sugar Factory."

"Hey, that's what I thought when I met my wife—excuse me, *ex*-wife," he corrected with a roll of his eyes. "'*She's not bad looking. She's great in the sack.*' Total marriage material, right?" he prompted before his expression changed instantly. "Wrong," he snapped. "Next thing I knew, she was sleeping with the handyman. So much for marriage material."

I had to laugh. "Right, because you *weren't* constantly cheating on her every chance you got?" I asked, absolutely knowing better. "Weren't you doing every female yoga in-structor at the Center at some point when your wife thought you were doing tai chi classes?"

Rob grinned. "Hey look, sometimes you can't change a

man's nature," he explained. "And me, I'm a hunter. Man was never meant to be monogamous. It's evolution. It's *scientific*," he declared, tapping his temple with his forefinger. "I'm just not meant to settle down with just one. No matter how hot the sex is." He put down his empty beer pint and raised his hand to order another. "Think about it," he proposed. "Eventually, there's going to be another girl who's even hotter. It's inevitable. Nothing lasts," he stated. "Nothing good anyway."

Not that I was buying into Rob's bitter, cynical, potentially sociopathic sales pitch, or taking to his particular shade of rose-colored outlook in life, but what he said did make me think.

I decided that what was bugging me was just that I had no closure. Especially since everything had ended not on my terms, but Claire's.

It was a simple case of wanting what I couldn't have. I couldn't possibly be actually pining over having a relationship. I wasn't about to change my bachelor ways and the life that I loved. Being a hunter was my nature too. I should just enjoy my big win and move on.

And maybe the reason I was so blown away by Claire was the same way diets worked.

Maybe it was like having a nice, juicy steak after not having meat for so long.

Before New Year's Eve, I had been holding myself back for weeks, so it stood to reason, I could have been not looking at it objectively.

Claire wasn't really *that* good. She was just "cheat day." And maybe I had been so focused on the "mission", all this confusion was just some residual energy that would eventually wear off.

With that all finally settled, I felt recharged. "You know what?" I finished my drink and prompted Rob, "Spot me another lap dance."

"That's what I'm talking about!" Rob clapped his hands, grinning as he raised his hand with mock formality. "Garçon!"

***

I got Marco and Nina's wedding invite in the mail in early March. And by then, I was all back to normal.

7

⧢

Marco and Nina's Wedding Registry

I wasn't the type of person who planned ahead. It was already May when I rummaged through my old mail to dig out the wedding invite, only then finally feeling compelled to go through the motions of preparing to attend the wedding, not to mention being a groomsman.

In fact, I hadn't even thought about the wedding for months.

An important contract had come up at work so I had been busier than usual, and I found that being busy with work didn't give me much time to think about personal stuff, which was probably all well and good. I definitely needed to clear the slate anyway.

But I didn't realize what being a groomsman at that

particular wedding entailed as there was certainly much less hoopla at Tyler's wedding.

Nor did I notice that my invitation had come with a schedule of such related activities—suit fittings, meetings with the bride and groom, seating chart discussions, planning the bachelor party.

Another sheet of paper that came with the invite spelled out options for another vital task that needed to be undertaken—what to buy the newlyweds as a wedding gift.

Marco and Nina had set up a wedding registry at Gump's, this fancy-ass store near Market Street. I was already passing it on the way back from a client meeting one afternoon, so I thought I might as well just get it over with.

Preparing for weddings was probably my weakest skill. Shopping for presents being a close second. I was just hoping that the registry wasn't all chick stuff—pink comforters and gravy boats.

I could have had that client meeting the day before or after. I could have decided to take a cab back to the office and skipped walking past Gump's altogether. But fate was a tricky thing.

Or maybe it was just plain old vengeful karma that I spotted Claire in the homeware section as soon as I came up the escalator.

The last time I had seen Claire was at *La Verde*, this upscale restaurant in the Financial District a couple of months ago. It looked like she was having a working lunch with some colleagues or clients. I was there with a date.

Even with Claire's intense, professional demeanor, just

scribbling down notes, and talking dispassionately with her group, I still thought she looked pretty hot.

But instead of being rattled, I had decided to focus on the superior thought that I had already "been there, done that."

I had wanted to come over and at least say "hi"—I mean, I still had manners, but let's just say my date had distracted me with something else.

Regardless, that afternoon at Gump's, it still felt like it had been so long, I wasn't prepared to see Claire all of a sudden. I thought I caught her gaze sweep past my direction and instinctively, I hunched, turning around, pretending to inspect something on the shelf.

But I was 6'4". It wasn't like I could hide.

"Alex?"

I turned around, a bit surprised that she had decided to speak to me first. I mean, she could have just left immediately. We hadn't even spoken for over four months. "Uh...hi." My mouth was dry. I cleared my throat and tried again. "Hi. Claire." I managed a plain smile.

"Hi." She paused for a moment, looking unsure what to say next then she noticed the piece of paper I was holding in recognition. "Ah, you've got Marco and Nina's gift registry too."

I looked down blankly at my hand. "Yeah." I nodded, only then noticing she had another copy in her hands. "So, you're still going to the wedding?" I asked, somewhat surprised.

"Of course," she said. It was subtle but I could tell there was still something in her eyes that was unsettled about the idea—even then. "Wow." She let out a slight chuckle. "It's really weird to run into you. It's been...a while."

Weird? That might not have been the word I would have

used. "You look—good." I wasn't sure exactly what I should say. But then I told myself that there was absolutely no reason I should be toning it down. I wasn't even entirely sure if we still were friends at all.

"Uh, thanks." Claire's smile looked a bit adorably lopsided. "Listen." She paused again, looking embarrassed. "I wanted to apologize for making you leave the group."

I was going to dismiss it but she stopped me.

"No, no," she continued. "Please. I was...an emotional wreck. I admit I didn't handle it very well." She met my gaze. "I know it might be four months too late but I wanted to tell you—I *am* sorry."

That made me smile. "I..." I hesitated. "I'm...sorry too." Except I wasn't really sorry. Admittedly, my goals with regards to Claire in the beginning might not have been too honorable but I felt like I wouldn't have changed a thing were it to happen all over again.

And as those big blue eyes looked up at me again, I felt a sudden twinge. And I knew, whatever I thought I had already resolved, regardless of how much time had passed, or how many philosophical platitudes I'd come up with, or even how many other girls had come and gone—despite everything, one thing was unquestionably clear.

I still wanted her.

It was a particularly unusual thought but I didn't say anything.

"And if it helps at all, everyone kept looking for you," Claire went on with a friendly smile. "They all missed you."

"Hm." I nodded in short acknowledgment with a hollow smile, noting that she didn't say 'we.' My unexpected realization had rendered me sort of speechless and I was try-ing to clear my head so I could re-establish my cool and calm façade but it caused a few moments of awkward silence.

Fortunately, Claire was up to par. "So, have you decided what to get the happy couple yet?" Her tone switched to casual and impersonal, as though she was a salesperson at Gump's, gesturing to the selection around us.

I shook my head, immeasurably relieved for the change in conversation topic. "Honestly, I was just going to get the first thing I managed to find in the store," I admitted.

When she smiled again, her eyes were soft. "Now, how did I know you were going to say that?"

Somehow, Marco and Nina's registry list facilitated as a great ice breaker, keeping the conversation between Claire and me focused on other matters. And even though we were both just begrudgingly shopping for wedding presents for our friends, I was having a good time.

Claire and I had never spent that kind of time together alone before. I supposed not being a big fan of Marco and Nina's wedding certainly gave us both some common ground. It actually surprised me how well we were getting along.

And when eventually Claire checked her wristwatch, she said, "Oh man, it's so late. I have to go."

I met her gaze evenly. But then she just smiled, and I mustered up a neutral smile in return. "I'll walk you home."

It seemed as though none of the stuff since New Year's Eve had happened and all the awkwardness between us was put aside and forgotten for a while as I walked Claire the eight or so blocks back to her apartment.

"And that thing they claimed was a kitchen tool—" Claire couldn't keep her laughter in as she tried to describe one of the items we had looked at earlier in the shop. "It looked like a screwdriver but the metal end of it was all twirly—even I couldn't tell what the hell it was."

I grinned myself as it had certainly been unidentifiable to me. "What's Nina going to do with all this stuff anyway?" I had to wonder then, wrinkling my nose as I read another line on the list. "I seriously doubt Marco wanted to have this 'twelve-piece antique hand-painted miniature Chinese tea set'."

Claire laughed again. "Oh come on, it's for Nina's miniature dollhouse," she quipped. "It probably matches her 'My Little Pony' collection perfectly."

I laughed out loud as well.

We had started a joke that Nina was a four-year-old girl based on her registry selections. The joke wasn't particularly clever but it was hilarious at the time.

"Aren't you glad you're not the one marrying Nina," Claire stated more than asked, elbowing me lightly.

"No, no." I shook my head at the preposterous idea. "Marco had called dibs. That was settled in the first two seconds."

"Oh, wow." She nodded, looking impressed. "Way to go, Marco."

"Besides—" I shrugged. "You know me. I make it clear to these women that I am absolutely not looking for a relationship."

"Yeah." She nodded again as she definitely knew all about

it. "I mean, the mere way you pick them up is already a clear red flag indicating that."

"Aw, come on," I chided. "Where's the fun in it otherwise? Don't you remember that time I pretended to be a single dad?" I asked her. "Man, I got laid so many times. That was a classic move."

Claire was already nodding but she had also started giggling so hard, she couldn't speak.

"Then one of the moms caught me out with the kid I was pretending was mine. I was so busted."

Claire finally took in enough air to manage to respond. "Oh, please. Of course, I remember that. I also remember that time when you pretended to be a cop. That's actually a felony, you know?"

I laughed again. "What? I don't even remember that one. But I guess sometimes I just get these strokes of brilliance. It makes me absolutely irresistible."

"You are *absolutely* repugnant." Claire shook her head in derision but it seemed more like mirth.

I shot her a curious look. "How do you even remember all that?"

"I am a lawyer," Claire replied.

"No, no." I feigned suspicion. "I knew it. You're running some kind of tally. Alex Keaton, number of rejections. And here I thought I was the only one keeping a list. This is so embarrassing."

Claire's jaw dropped eagerly. "I knew it. There's actually a list, isn't there?" she prompted. "I've just won a bet with Janice."

I shot her a strange amused look but before I could let her

know I was obviously just kidding, she said something next that surprised me.

"Seriously Alex, as someone who's actually *on* this list, all I'm hoping is that I'm ranked the worst on it," Claire remarked. "At least, it would speak to your good taste in women, if not your delicacy."

"Um." I wasn't sure how to reply. After all this time, trust Claire to bring it up again in such an unaffected, neutral, almost comical way. I tried to be light-hearted about it as well. "There is no such list, Claire," I told her. "But rest assured if there was, your name would have a big star next to it. Most difficult, but absolutely most worth the effort," I said, in no way lying.

"Oh, don't try to flatter me now." She waved dismissively. "Surely, any number of these women were far better than *little ol' me*," she said with a mimicked accent.

I looked at her, amazed. Claire was just so engaging and funny... And she had such a strength and confidence about her that I just couldn't help but be awed by.

My thoughts strayed back to New Year's Eve. Maybe Claire was also thinking about that night. Maybe after having been gone for so long, she *had* actually missed me. I mean, she was the one who approached me this afternoon. She could have said no when I offered to walk her home. She hadn't been wary around me all evening. In fact, I thought if anything, she was even responding to me.

Maybe after all this time, she had somehow come around to reconsider. And *maybe*—maybe she wanted *me* too... The thought made my heart pound all over again.

"Here we go." Claire's voice broke into my thoughts and I

looked up at the homey three-story pastel-colored apartment building before following her up the steps to the front door. "I'm so sorry you felt like you had to walk me home," she apologized with a slight laugh as she fished out her keys from her purse.

A corner of my mouth turned up in a slight smile. I had kept myself in check all afternoon, but after what had felt oddly like a date, I was wondering how the evening was going to end. I discreetly glanced up at her apartment window upstairs, trying to forcibly shake the thought out of my mind. Except my pulse was already racing in anticipation and I was starting to breathe heavily.

I thought about New Year's Eve again. What were the odds that what had happened that night between us was just a fluke? Surely, that was a theory that needed testing. Closure or not, I was also starting to wonder if maybe I was actually more into her than I'd initially thought.

I dismissed that notion fast. *Stop it. That's ridiculous.* What was more likely was that I just couldn't let that one night of perfect sex go without a reprise.

I swallowed hard, watching her turn the key and open the door.

Then she looked back up at me with those eyes.

Just one kiss, my mind screamed. I was staring down at her mouth. I wanted to stroke her full red bottom lip with my thumb, cup her face in my hands, dig my fingers up into her hair from the nape of her neck... It had been four whole months. I couldn't believe how much I wanted her right then.

"Alex...?"

And the way she spoke my name sent shivers up my spine

as I remembered how she had moaned it in bed and all my control crumbled.

***

I collapsed on my back against the bed, out of breath and bewildered all over again.

Nope. No fluke.

Claire was absolutely completely hot. Being with her was like nothing else I'd ever known. I couldn't stop wanting more.

Claire sat up in bed again, except this time I heard her let out a little nervous laugh. "Well," she began. "You're still incredible. Oh my god."

I felt like my grin would crack my face in half. *Still...?*

If that wasn't a compliment, I didn't know what was. I sat up to nuzzle her bare shoulder, my fingers in her hair, my lips moving up the side of her neck as I murmured, "You—are absolutely perfect."

She moved away, ticklish, with a slight giggle, before she let out a soft groan. "Ohh, you're exactly what I need to get through this wedding."

I was slightly puzzled, not yet fully understanding what she meant, but I didn't press. I was still much too elated that she hadn't rushed to kick me out the door after two minutes.

I watched her get up from bed, reach for a dressing gown off a hook beside the closet, and put it on. Her movements were so graceful. I leaned back on my elbows in bed, just enjoying watching her.

Claire leaned over to check a little clock by her dressing

table. "Oh wow," she remarked at the time. "I'm glad I told Janice I was busy working this week. Otherwise, she would have been expecting me at the bar."

"Hey." I smoothed back my hair as I sat up again. "Maybe tomorrow, we skip the bar and have dinner at that new ramen place, the one that always has a long line outside," I began. "We can get there ridiculously early and you know, wait." I smiled suggestively.

I was still smiling because I was definitely not expecting a rejection. But then she replied.

"Oh, no I can't. I have a date tomorrow," she said, tying up her hair into a careless ponytail.

I blinked, somewhat taken aback. "Oh."

"Yeah, I'm sort of seeing someone," she said with a casual shrug.

That felt like another punch in the face. I dropped my gaze to the sheets I was still tangled in in bed, a disturbing realization dawning on me.

"Hey, uh, I assume we're already on the same page, but what just happened—" She gestured to the two of us. "It stays between us, right?"

I snapped out of it enough to respond. "Uh, y-yeah, of course."

Claire smiled, reaching toward the nightstand for my phone, proceeding to put her number in under a codename, like any old booty-call on speed dial. Then she leaned over me in bed to kiss me again.

I reached my hand up to touch her face but she pulled away right after just a brief kiss.

"Alright," she said casually. "I'm going to hop into the shower. You can let yourself out, right Alex?"

I hadn't even managed to reply before she disappeared into the bathroom.

I shook my head briskly to clear it before I stood up to gather my clothes and got dressed back up again. I thought about waiting for Claire to step out of the shower first before leaving so I could say goodbye but then decided against it. And within a few minutes, I was back outside in the cold. I shoved my hands in my pockets and headed home.

What the hell just happened?

I was sure I was supposed to be happy with the sudden unexpected turn of events.

Then I forcibly pushed all my confusion aside.

That was, *of course* I was happy with the turn of events. This was even better than what I had initially planned. What other guy in town could boast the booty-call number of the gorgeous Claire Hale on their phone?

But actually, I never got to use it.

Mostly because Claire always seemed to beat me to it.

I didn't want to seem presumptuous. In fact, the first time she had called me up to come over, I'd even brought over a bottle of wine, thinking it was a social call.

But Claire, bless her soul, was all about the business.

Not to mention, she was totally addictive. Like I would seriously ditch another girl in the middle of fooling around just to go hook up with Claire. It was almost ludicrous.

Hooking up with Claire felt like heaven and hell. Not counting work and wedding preps, it was the best—and worst —two weeks of my life.

8

Marco and Nina's
Week Of

I walked into *The Irish* after what had felt like ages to attend a "bridal party meeting" instigated by Nina. I was already planning to go even without Marco saying he wouldn't take no for an answer.

With the wedding only a week away, I could just imagine that Marco and Nina were probably in an all-the-time all-wedding frenzy by then.

I also thought it was finally safe to come out of hiding. Even if I knew Claire would most likely be there too, I had the feeling that she was all ready to lift my exile order. I had been seeing her on and off for the past few weeks already anyway. What was one night?

Naturally, my arrival was an event of some peculiarity and wonder.

"Well, look what the cat dragged in," Marco mused aloud.

"Hey! Alex! You're here! What a surprise!" Janice greeted brightly.

"The prodigal son returns. Where have you been, bro?" Tyler asked, waving me over. "You disappeared into the woodwork."

"Yes, yes, I'm back. We'll have a group hug later, okay?" I dismissed nonchalantly, briefly noting that Claire had not arrived yet.

Admittedly, I felt eager to catch up with everyone after so long. And it was highly entertaining to meet Nina's two hot blonde bridesmaids, Bridgette and Alyssa from her college sorority, who were both absolutely thrilled to meet me.

"Dude, it feels like we haven't seen you in a year. Where the heck have you been?" Marco prompted, thumping on my back good-naturedly as I sat down in the booth.

"Just working," I replied, as it was the hardly debatable response.

"You've missed two bridal party meetings so far," Nina informed me as she pulled out her phone to check a list of some type. "Aaand it looks like you haven't shown up for suit fittings yet either, or picked out a task to do for the day itself from my shortlist—"

"Whoa." I was a little bit disoriented to hear Nina sounding so organized, but then I mistakenly added, "Is someone being a bridezilla already?"

"Ohh!" Tyler, Janice, Alyssa, and Bridgette cheered as Nina's eyes widened.

I looked around, startled, clueless. "What? What?"

"We've started a game," Bridgette explained. "Well, actually,

Nina made us start a game. Any time someone refers to her as a bridezilla—" She reached under the table to retrieve something before standing up to walk over to me. "They get to wear this *gorgeous* veil," she said, plunking something on my head.

I grimaced then carelessly flipped the back of the cheap veil fabric with my hand. "Matches my hair," I remarked, making everyone laugh again and I turned back to Marco. "Well, from the sounds of it then, I'm glad I wasn't around to be tortured like this," I joked.

"Are you freaking kidding me? You didn't make it to my awesome engagement party, you jackass," Marco reprimanded. "And just when I'd managed to get that DJ we found in Daytona during spring break, remember him? He was like freaking van Buuren. He was super awesome! And then you totally flaked out on me, man—"

"What's going on?"

I looked up when I heard Claire's voice as she seemed to just materialize out of the bar crowd.

She gave me a look. "Is Alex the blushing bride today?" she prompted with a smirk, noting my awesome veil.

My eyes lit up and I was going to retort something playful back when I noticed another guy materialize out of the same bar crowd from behind her before he settled beside Claire to casually sling his arm around her shoulders. My smile faded at once.

"Oh, hey, Wayne." Janice gave him a quick wave. "Guys, shift down." She motioned for Tyler and me to make space in the booth for Claire and 'Wayne.'

And before anyone else could get another word out, Nina

spoke up. "Claire, great, you're here," she said. "Finally, we're complete, for once."

I zoned out as soon as Nina started to talk about wedding stuff. I glanced over at Claire and Wayne again. For some reason, I couldn't help but instantly hate the guy.

Obviously, I'd seen Claire with boyfriends in the past. They had always just barely registered on my radar.

That night, however, I couldn't help but notice that Wayne was clearly not as good-looking as I was, nor as tall, nor as charming, nor better dressed. I gritted my teeth. And if he was an architect, I was going to choke somebody. But I forcibly shook the thought off and tried to focus on something else.

Alyssa was making eyes at me across the table.

I managed to give her a tight smile in response.

I could already tell that I would have no problems getting Alyssa, or even Bridgette, to sleep with me. But instead of thinking about that, or listening to the usher duties that Nina was doling out, I couldn't stop thinking about the mind-blowing sex that this Wayne guy was probably going to have later that night.

"Bro." Tyler elbowed me.

"What?"

Nina's eyebrows were raised in a prompt as she looked at me. "Tomorrow please, suit fittings. Do *not* miss it," she said in a surprisingly firm, almost threatening tone.

I pursed my lips to stifle my chuckle and just nodded. "Uh, yes ma'am," I replied. I glanced over at Marco who was just shaking his head at me in amusement and I tossed my veil at him, making him laugh. I laughed too, despite noting somewhat skeptically how happy he looked.

And for the first time, in spite of myself, I noticed that the way they were doing their "couple talk" and ending each other's sentences was actually proof of how supportive and in-synch they were with each other.

I cracked a smirk, surprised, amused, impressed—slightly annoyed too, but still sort of impressed.

When the "official meeting" ended, Nina and her bridesmaids had to leave to take care of some bachelorette party planning and Marco happily walked them to the door.

I watched Marco leave with them before looking over at Tyler. "Can you believe that guy?" I prompted. "It's like he has to ask Nina for permission to stay behind to hang out with his friends."

But Janice was the one to reply. "Hey, he's in love," she reprimanded. "Leave him alone."

Claire decided to make a wry joke. "I think Alex is jealous."

Tyler and Janice laughed and I shot Claire a curious look but she had turned to Wayne to explain the situation. "Alex is Marco's BFF," she relayed even as she shot a mischievous glance back at me.

I rolled my eyes when Wayne chuckled. "Whatever happened to 'bros before hoes'? It was such a noble idea." I shook my head as I reached my hand out across the way toward Wayne. "Dude, we haven't officially met. I'm Alex."

He shook my hand. "Wayne Pemberton. Good to meet you," he replied.

I nodded slowly. "Right." I resisted the urge to ask him

more questions but it felt important to keep staring at him until he looked away.

Wayne cleared his throat and leaned over toward Claire. "Do you need another drink?"

She smiled at him in reply. "Yeah," she said, standing up with him. "Hey, we'll just get the next round, you guys."

Tyler stood up himself. "Hey, wait up for me," he called out.

That made Janice snicker. "Ty wants to try out this girly drink and he knows there is no way in hell I'm going to order it for him," she told me.

"Right." I chuckled at that, my gaze distracting up toward Claire at the bar a couple of times.

But Janice was watching me and she gave me a calculating narrow-eyed look. "I know that look."

I blinked, looking away. "What look?"

"That's your getting-ready-to-pounce look." Her jaw dropped. "Oh my god, you're thinking of hitting on Claire," she accused. Then she pointedly added, "Don't do it."

I shot her a shocked look. "Please Janice," I drawled. "I'm not thinking anything like that. Besides, Claire's with Wayne. And, as you know, she would *never* in a million years," I said emphatically. "Seriously, that all sounds so very, very, very, *very* un-Claire-like," I concluded with a shake of my head, hoping I had hyperbole'd enough.

But Janice let it go easily with a firm nod. "Well, good," she said. "Wayne's pretty nice. You'd better not mess it up."

I paused, furrowing my eyebrows in thought. *Mess it up?* As if somehow Janice was implying that Claire would be getting a raw deal if I got involved and she lost Wayne. *Was he even good enough for her?*

Admittedly, I'd only been interested in going straight to the finish line with Claire. I'd never even really tried to just ask her out. And just then I wondered if Janice also thought I wasn't good enough for Claire either. The thought wasn't particularly encouraging.

Claire came back to the booth as the guys were waiting on the drinks to arrive at the counter but she didn't sit down. It looked like she was headed for the restrooms.

And the ever-so-helpful Janice decided to give her a heads up. "Claire, you watch out for this guy," she pointed out loudly, gesturing to me. "I think he's trying to sleep with you," she said, fully in jest, not realizing how accurate she was being.

Too late for that, I thought, my lips pursed as I met Claire's gaze to check her reaction.

But Claire just laughed. "Oh Janice," she mumbled, shaking her head. "Would you give me a little credit?" was all she said before turning to head toward the back of the bar.

Except I caught her little glance back at me first and I straightened up, my pulse beginning to race immediately in understanding.

I was on.

Tyler had come back to the booth, giving me an opportunity to sneak off to the back without Janice noticing. And as soon as I turned down the hall, I was unable to bite back my smile.

Claire was at the end of the hall past the restrooms, leaning against the open doorway to the bar's isolated back kitchen area. She was waiting for me.

"Hi," she greeted me, this time with a smile, as I approached her.

"Hi." Seeing her smile made mine widen.

"Can you believe Janice?" She chuckled, making a face. "Do you think she would just literally explode if we tell her the truth?"

"Uh, yeah, I would imagine she would." I cleared my throat, still sort of unsettled after that warning from Janice. "So, is that guy with you—"

"Wayne."

I stopped short. "Wayne, right," I went on. "Is that the same guy you went out with last week?"

She nodded. "Yeah, he's really nice," she relayed as she walked up closer to me. She furtively looked around to make sure nobody could see us before deftly pushing me into the kitchen. Then she slid her hands up my chest and behind my neck, making me shiver again before she pulled my head down for a kiss.

She dug her fingers through my hair and I felt instantly warm all over.

I put my arms around her, spinning to lift her up onto the counter, kissing her back. But I couldn't concentrate. "So," I murmured against her mouth. "What's up with this Wayne guy?"

"I don't know. He's nice," she replied, her arms around my neck, still kissing me.

"Have you had sex with him yet?"

She stopped short, stunned, pulling away to look at me. "What?"

I frowned. "So, what is it—are you cheating on him with me?"

"Of course not, silly." She shook her head. "He knows we're not exclusive."

I met her gaze, bracing my hands on her arms. "Is this what we're doing?" I paused for a long second, furrowing my eyebrows. "What *are* we doing?"

Claire laughed lightly. "I just wanted to say hi. Lighten up, Alex." She leaned up to kiss me again and I closed my eyes, letting her sweetness wash over me. But then she broke off with a, "I should get back to Wayne."

"Hey." I held her fast, my frown deepening with the sudden constriction in my chest. "Why don't you just be with me tonight?" I coaxed huskily. I was trying to sound casual about it but for some reason, I was feeling unexpectedly possessive.

But Claire's laughter just trailed off as she looked up at me as if to tell me that she could tell I wasn't serious. "You'd better go back first," she merely instructed, unlatching my arms from around her waist.

I was still frowning when I got back to the booth at the same time as Marco, Wayne, and Tyler were bringing back a pitcher and some bottles. I blinked distractedly, looking up at them.

Then Claire walked back to the booth, looking as normal as worldly possible.

"Hey Claire," Wayne started. "I actually have an early start tomorrow so I think I should head off."

Claire straightened up as well. "Oh, hey, you know what?" She shot Janice a pointed look. "I think these two," she said, gesturing to Marco and Tyler. "Have missed their little boyfriend," she went on with a grin, obviously referring to me. "Let's just all leave them alone. Come on, Janice." She took her arm to escort her away. "Wayne and I will drop you off home."

But I was still reeling a bit from the spur-of-the-moment covert make-out session with Claire.

Don't get me wrong. I knew the score.

Claire was obviously just using me as a distraction away from Marco and Nina's wedding. That was what I wanted too. And I'd had absolutely no qualms about it. But that night, seeing her with Wayne, I was feeling a little less than elated about the arrangement.

I watched Claire all the while until the three of them had gone, kind of left hanging, almost feeling that somehow I missed her already. And that I *really* hated that guy.

But Tyler was eager to begin his interview as if it had been orchestrated. "Alright, seriously, Alex, now that the girls are gone, where *have* you been?" he wanted to know.

I shrugged big. "Nowhere. I told you."

"Look, you've been gone for months. That's not something you can just shrug off. I think we both know you a little better," Marco pointed out as he refilled his pint.

I tilted my head, slightly uncomfortable with the line of questioning. "I just...I *really was* busy with work," I insisted.

"Uh-huh." Tyler gave me a look. "What's her name?"

I let out a laugh, managing to cover my nerve. "Tracy, Alicia, Monique, Natasha. Take your pick."

"Dude," Marco began meaningfully. "It's us. You can tell us whatever it is—oh shoot." He picked up his ringing phone almost instantaneously. "It's Nina," he said and left the table to head toward the front door to take the call.

I pursed my lips, leaning back against my seat in disbelief. "Thanks, dude!" I called out. "Good talk."

Tyler chuckled. "I think Claire was right."

I paused warily. "Why?"

"I think you *should* be jealous of Nina," he said with a grin.

I sighed heavily, mostly in mirth.

Maybe they were both right. For sure, I was missing my wingman. I'd never really had a *best* friend in my life, but Marco was the closest thing I had. We had barely hung out in the past few months. And he was getting married next week, moving on with his life. Maybe he would be so busy with married life that we wouldn't see each other anymore. *Everything* was about to change.

And maybe all of this was shining a huge spotlight on how small and empty my life might be viewed in comparison that the insecurity was manifesting in all this chaos regarding Claire.

And maybe after all the wedding craziness passed, Claire and I would just simply part ways and agree that this was the best distraction ever. Like, of all time.

Tyler's chuckle trailed off and he began again more seriously. "Look, if it's a matter of you don't have anyone else to talk to since Marco is off spinning in wedding planning world at the moment that he wouldn't notice if a meteor crash-landed on the bar right now—honestly, just let me know," he assured, patting my back.

I almost laughed again. I honestly didn't know what the hell was going on either.

Regardless, Tyler was definitely right about one thing. Whatever the hell it was, the absolute last person I could tell was Marco.

9

❧

Nina's Bachelorette Party

Or rather, the morning after Nina's Bachelorette Party.

I half-opened my eyes, just on the brink of waking up, and was stunned for a split second.

Claire's light brown hair was half-buried under my pristine white sheets as she lay, still asleep, beside me in bed.

I blinked a few times but not moving otherwise, the events of the previous night all coming back to me.

Claire had shown up drunk at my door in the middle of the night. She had come from Nina's bachelorette party and the two of us had fallen into bed again.

I sighed heavily, rolling over to face the ceiling.

Usually, the random one-night stand that I brought back to my apartment would have been long gone in the early hours of the morning. If not, I would have already dropped all the hints required for them to do so, short of kicking them out the door.

But this was Claire.

The last time she was here was New Year's Eve and she had bolted out the door after two minutes.

I didn't understand what was going on with me but I'd had enough of a headache trying to figure it out all week. I was sick of thinking. All I knew for the moment was that I didn't feel the need to get up and make up an excuse to disappear post-haste. And I didn't mind waking up next to Claire.

I turned slightly to reach over to brush the hair back from her face.

"Mm…" Claire murmured, her eyes fluttering open as she woke. "Alex…?"

A corner of my mouth curled up involuntarily. At least she remembered whose bed she was in well enough. "Morning," I said under my breath.

But then her forehead creased, her eyes squeezing shut again, and she groaned out loud. "Oh man!" she moaned. "My head is pounding."

That made me laugh.

Claire had a terrible hangover.

"Ohh, sssshhhh!!" she shushed loudly, burying her head under the pillow. "Aspirin!"

I stifled my laughter as I carefully got up, patting her back. "Stay here. I'll go get you something," I said, barely above a whisper.

"Shut up, Alex—you're so loud!" Her groan was partially muffled by the pillow.

I shook my head in amusement as I headed toward the kitchen.

The days coming to Marco and Nina's wedding were rushing on by.

I had finally dutifully completed all my groomsman tasks. My suit had been fitted and was hanging in my closet. Registry gift selected, wrapped up, and sent. I had done my part of Nina's bidding regarding her other wedding errands. And tomorrow, everyone was flying off to Vegas for the wedding that weekend.

I honestly didn't know whether or not I was relieved to be getting the wedding over and done with.

I had been back hanging out at the bar with the guys for the past few nights, even as Claire and I were still doing the down-low, sneaking around. But who knew, without the wedding to be distracted from, these could be the last few days that we were going to be hooking up.

I came back to the room with a glass of water and a bottle of Gatorade.

Claire opened one eye to peek up at me from beneath the pillow. "Where's the aspirin?"

I sat on the edge of the bed beside her. "This is better," I chided lightly. "Don't worry. I can tell a major hangover when I see one and trust me, I am highly experienced with hangovers, having had so many myself."

She wrinkled her nose up at me, slowly pushing herself up, wrapping the bed sheet up around her torso as she did. "Steer into the skid, huh?" she asked, reaching out her hand for the bottle.

I chuckled under my breath. "Always." I stroked her back.

Claire smirked a little. "Thanks, Alex." She shook her head just then. "I'm so sorry. I know girls don't usually stay this long in your apartment. I promise I'll be out the door just as soon as I can get my bearings."

I made a face, a bit weirded out that she was concerned about that. "Look, you take your time, alright?" I advised. "I'll go see if I can find something to eat."

I was making some toast in the kitchen when I heard some thumping and moving around at the other end of the hall. I stopped.

"Claire," I called out, raising my eyebrow curiously. "You okay back there?"

And when I walked back to the room, I almost ran into her coming out, at the same time as she was trying to zip up the back of the red dress she had been wearing last night, carrying her matching high heels by their straps in her other hand.

I gave her a surprised look. "What are you doing?"

She gave me a sheepish look. "I really should go," she replied, even as she was making a face, likely caused by her splitting headache.

I gave her a firm pointed look. "No." I turned her around to head back into the room. "Claire, you are hung over. You need to stay and rest and eat something. Now, don't make me tear that dress off of you again, 'cause I admit I totally enjoyed that last night," I quipped with a grin.

Claire's grimace shifted as she laughed. "Fine!" She sighed resignedly. "Saves me having to return this dress," she joked.

"Look, if you're feeling up to it, you can go have a quick shower," I told her, pointing toward the bathroom. "You can grab some clothes from the closet. There should be some flannels in the back."

"Oh, you mean I can't borrow one of your Dolce suits to

throw up in?" she asked mischievously and I shot her a deadpan warning look. But she just laughed. "Alright already, Mr. Bossy." She rolled her eyes, shooing me out of the room.

I grabbed a plain white t-shirt as I headed back to the kitchen, shaking my head, mostly in mirth. I couldn't help but feel particularly light. I was finding Claire's company unexpectedly settling and it felt good to be in charge for a change. I smiled to myself as I sliced some fruit.

I heard Claire run the shower for a few minutes and when she finished, I heard some more thumps and rummaging and I assumed she was looking for those flannel shirts.

Then I heard her call out, "What's all this?" from inside the room.

I glanced up. I couldn't see her from the kitchen. "What's what?" I replied loudly, not moving from the kitchen.

"*What's what?*" she echoed in ridicule. "This mountain of boxes that I have to climb over in your closet to get to your cheap-ass clothes section."

My eyes widened as I remembered. "Oh, jeez, right," I replied. "Sorry about that mess. My mom sent me some boxes of my stuff. She's finally selling our old house. Are you—" I tried to crane my neck to see down the hall since I was almost elbow-deep in fruit peel. "Do you need me to—?"

Then I heard more thumping. "Nah, I'm fine," she called out. Then I saw her poke her head out of the room doorway in time to meet my gaze from the kitchen. "Aww!" She gave me a pout. "Cute dog!"

I stifled my laughter, assuming that she had found a framed photo of my old dog, Bunker, among the boxes.

She poked her head back into the room. "I can't imagine

my folks ever selling our old place," she remarked loudly so I could hear. "I mean, selling the house you grew up in. That must feel weird, huh—all those childhood memories?"

"Yeah." I shrugged nonchalantly, replying in turn. "Not really. I actually barely grew up there 'cause you know, right after the divorce..." I trailed off, slightly uncomfortable.

But I didn't have to finish. She knew. "That's right," she said, suddenly subdued. "Your dad died."

I stopped chopping for a moment at the memory before I blew out a breath to shake it off. "Yeah, so Mom's moving down to some condo in San Diego with Mr. Pilot Man #3." I switched tones, trying to make a joke out of it.

"Mm," I heard Claire murmur absently. She poked her head out of the room again briefly to give me a funny expression as she held up a yellowed bandanna. "Alex, seriously?" she prompted skeptically. "You were a boy scout?"

I shot her a narrow-eyed look. "Yes," I replied, trying not to look embarrassed. "And I was a damn good one," I added, knowing all my badges and certificates were in the same pile in the box.

Then after a beat, she called out something, "Did you just print these out too?"

"Thanks a lot." I shook my head. "What are you even rummaging around in there for?"

"I don't know. I'm curious. Who was the guy in these boxes? He seems kinda cool."

I stiffened. "Well...I'm different now." I was torn between bragging about all of my old sports medals and trophies and being self-conscious from how the hard evidence of a somewhat meager version of myself might appear to Claire.

But I dismissed the thought again, trying to wave her away pointedly, even though she couldn't see me. "Look, stop snooping around in there. That's personal."

"Okay, but not before you tell me about being the 'Chippiest Chipper at Kipper Clothiers' for...five, six, *seven* months in a row—" she relayed, sounding highly amused. "Whatever happened to the eighth month, Alex?"

I made a face, my jaw dropping in exasperation. "Seriously, Claire," I called out firmly. "Get out of my stuff!"

Her melodious laugh echoed down the hallway and I looked up in time to see her shadowy figure come out of the room.

"If you must know," I informed her. "That was my first job, and on month eight, I got a promotion. Not all of us were borne of money like Mr. Marco Welling," I remarked offhand, whom in hindsight I probably should not have brought up since the mention of him changed the entire expression on Claire's face for a moment as she came out to the kitchen.

But I was stopped short, struck by how stunning she still looked wearing my big plaid flannel shirt. Claire's beauty was absolutely effortless. She took my breath away and for a moment I couldn't say anything.

But then Claire's gaze fell on the kitchen counter and her expression changed again, to shock this time. "Wha—what—?" She couldn't even complete her question but she recovered quickly, wryly. "Exactly how many hungover girls have you got hiding in your apartment right now?" she wanted to know. "You look like you're about to feed an army!"

I blinked at the counter and dismissed it. "It's just toast and some fruit." A *lot* of fruit. I guessed I hadn't realized how much I had started to prepare. "Well, I'm eating too anyway," I said, popping an orange slice in my mouth.

She let out a light laugh as she came up to the counter beside me to survey the options, then she reached for a piece of toast and took a bite before walking off and wandering into the lounge.

I washed my hands, watching her take in the space for the first time.

"Why don't you put up some of those pictures your mom sent? Look at this place." She gestured around the very bare lounge. "At least make it look like an actual human being lives here."

"Aw, thanks, Claire." I put my hand to my chest, pretending to be touched as I followed her into the lounge. "You finally acknowledged that I'm a human being."

Her eyes lit up before she took off back toward the room and when she came back, the framed photo of a ten-year-old me and Bunker was in her hand. She pointedly plunked the picture on the center of my otherwise empty living room bookshelf.

I shook my head again in silent laughter. "Claire, this is *not* your apartment."

But she just pursed her lips, looking triumphant before she walked past the shelf and spotted a book on the coffee table. She let out a short laugh, sounding amused, as she picked it up. "I remember this." It was the Carl Sagan book that she had given me a long time ago. She nodded bemusedly, noting the bookmark I had used was wedged into some one-third of the book. "And I see you're still in the middle of reading this book I gave you—*four years ago*."

"Oh." I sheepishly walked up to take the book from her. "Actually, I finished it last spring. I'm just reading it again, 'cause there were some things I didn't understand." I shoved the book up on the shelf beside the photo frame.

She looked at me as though in astonished disbelief, then she gave me a weird wrinkled-nose look, swallowing her mouthful before she started to turn away, I assumed toward the kitchen to get some more food.

But I caught her shoulder lightly to stop her, coming closer. My heart started to pound in my chest again and she looked up to meet my gaze, almost questioningly.

I studied her eyes for a moment, then when I lifted my hand up to touch her face, she moved to press her cheek against my palm. The gesture was so sweet, I felt my chest constrict before I leaned down to cover her lips with mine.

And as I kissed her, there was something nagging in the back of my mind, as though something deeply repressed screaming to get out, perhaps something I didn't even want to admit to myself.

I broke off, a bit disoriented, and gestured back to the kitchen. "Um, there's also tomato juice in the fridge," I began. "It's...a great cure for hangovers."

But Claire's mouth turned up in a slight smirk. "You know what else is a great cure for hangovers?" she asked, raising her eyebrow.

"What?" I prompted, except I realized what the answer was as soon as I'd asked.

She simply grinned in reply, already helping me out of my t-shirt.

And we did it again. Twice.

I was careful not to wake Claire up as I went out to the balcony with the rest of her bottle of Gatorade. I glanced back at her through the window, feeling a massive disquiet. I blew out a heavy sigh as I turned to look out to the city.

All I needed to do was close my eyes and I could see Claire's face. Whenever we were together, all I ever wanted to do was to make her smile. And I always felt at ease around Claire, like there was never any need to pretend to be more or less of who I was.

Then again, maybe it was the knowledge that Claire expected absolutely nothing more from me that was particularly liberating. Otherwise, everything with her just seemed so...*simple*.

I shook my head briskly to clear it. *Jesus Christ.* I was starting to sound like Tyler. What was Claire trying to do to me? And why the hell was I letting her? I felt absolutely ill-equipped to even be having some of these thoughts.

It felt like such a cliché scene from the movies. I was imagining how Claire would walk out to the balcony, put her arms around me from behind, and tell me I was the only man she would ever want to be with. And for some reason, I found that thought oddly pleasing.

I sighed again, blinking out of my trance.

I heard a soft creak and I whirled around to see if it was Claire coming out to see me. But the balcony door was still shut.

I peered in through the glass to try to see.

The bed was empty. Claire had left.

10

Marco's Bachelor Party

"Well, one thing is definitely clear," Tyler said to me at the end of the night. "I'm glad I didn't get you to plan my bachelor party."

Gambling, cigars, booze, high-class—if not a bit on the racy end type of—entertainment, as well as, I had scored the most awesome penthouse strip club venue on The Strip.

All the best for Marco's legendary bachelor party.

I had to laugh, looking around as the rest of the guys were dispersing toward the exits. I saw Marco across the way saying goodbye and having some last-minute chats with some people.

"Hey," I reminded Tyler. "I distinctly remember having had a good time at your bachelor party too, even with your super strict, *super stupid* 'no strippers' rule," I said with a roll of my eyes.

"Well, of course, you did," he pointed out ruefully. "Because you managed to hook up with the catering chick." He shook his head. "I seriously don't know how you do it sometimes. Personally, I would be so exhausted getting chased by all these girls, man."

With those sorts of comments, I usually chuckle in satisfaction. Except for this time, I had to blow out a breath in exasperated agreement.

Tyler had no idea how my day had actually gone. The entire bridal party, and then some, had all flown into Vegas together, and I had spent all afternoon in the casino trying to fend off advances made by Alyssa and Bridgette and a couple of Nina's other sorority sisters.

Normally I wouldn't have given it a second thought but I just wasn't feeling it that day. And besides, something about being in Vegas just drove these girls nuts.

It was also made slightly worse since Claire had brought Wayne along as her plus one to the wedding. And he kept letting her through doors first and pulling out her chair like a damn gentleman, and pissing me the hell off.

My only reprieve was when the girls finally all had to go to their spa appointment at the hotel and I had to get everything ready for the bachelor party.

"Dudes!" Marco called out as he came back to our table, plunking himself between Tyler and me. "Now was that a party or *was that* a party?" he asked, sounding a bit giddy as he downed his *nth* bottle of beer.

"Oh man, good luck with him," Tyler told me as he finished his drink and started to stand up. "I'm afraid this old married man will have to retire now before the wife thinks I actually enjoyed this."

"Oh boo!" Marco hissed at him. "You suck, Ty."

I chuckled. "Thanks a lot, Ty."

Tyler wiggled his eyebrows at me. "Don't you boys stay out too late," he bid before he turned to leave.

I groaned in exhaustion as I turned to Marco. "Marco, man." I patted his back. "How about we play a little game of shut-eye next?" I started to stand.

"No, no, hey, I say one more drink. Come on, Alex. You owe me, man. You owe me," Marco told me.

I shot him a look. "Oh, for what?"

"You skipped out on a lot of my awesome parties this year," he reminded me, starting to slur a bit. "You disappeared for like months. You owe me so many beers and drinks. Waiter!" he called out. "Two more beers!"

I sighed, begrudgingly sitting back down to wait for the beers.

Naturally, I'd seen Marco super drunk before. It was almost a tradition between the two of us to take turns getting shit-faced. That way, the (mostly) sober one would always manage to keep us both out of trouble. It (mostly) worked.

And that night, Marco was at an all-time-high level of drunkenness. His clothes had beer stains on them and his hair was completely disheveled, combining sweat with undoubtedly more beer.

I settled back in my seat to watch him as I couldn't, for the life of me, comprehend what the hell it was about Marco that had Claire so damn hooked that she would need both me and Wayne to get over him. Like, what in the flipping world could Marco Welling possibly have that I did not?

"What's so great about you anyway?" I asked, suddenly and annoyingly inexplicably jealous of him.

"What?" Marco turned to ask.

I shook my head quickly to dismiss my ire. "I mean," I rephrased graciously. "How are you holding up? You're getting married in two days—" I stopped short to glance at my phone clock, seeing that it was past midnight. "Check that, tomorrow!"

Marco wheezed. "It's awesome, man. Everything's awesome right now."

I gave him a measured look. "No second thoughts?"

The beers arrived and he took a swig of one, shaking his head swiftly before he asked, "Why? Nina is the hottest thing on the planet. And she loves me."

I frowned. *So simple.* I took a deep breath. "That's great, man. Good for you."

"I mean, you know," Marco went on. "Sure our apartment has too many pink things," he remarked, making me smirk. "But she's the only one for me. I knew it right away."

I watched him for a moment, narrow-eyed. "How did you know?" I asked, a little more than curious.

"She's totally hot!" Marco exclaimed.

"Yeah, but so is Claire—" I stopped short, having not meant to say that.

"Claire?" Marco looked surprised at the mention.

"Uh, yeah." I tried to cover up my slip. "Didn't you...also go out before?"

"Claire, Claire, Claire." Marco had more beer. He shrugged. "Well, you know Claire. Claire is great. Maybe a little too serious, like she would just never get my jokes, you know?"

I tilted my head slightly, wanting to respond. *Well, that's because Claire's humor is intricate and clever.* But Marco went on.

"She has her moments though," he added with a suggestive wiggle of his eyebrows at me. "Why? Are you planning to hit that? I wouldn't blame you. I have *very* good memories of Claire. Especially in the sack, whoo—she makes a real effort."

I didn't realize I was gritting my teeth. *Dude, your information is four years old.* As clearly, Claire was now an expert in the sack. I resisted the powerful urge to say anything more.

"And if you're worried about me, don't be. You two crazy kids totally have my blessing."

"It's not like that." I shook my head again, trying to dismiss it and change the subject.

I absolutely didn't want any more details about his and Claire's sexual exploits. And for some reason, I didn't want the knowledge that Marco was absolutely fine with me hitting that. Somehow I felt like having Marco's blessing implied too much right then.

"Look," I started pointedly. "We better make a move. You look like shit."

"I have this theory. Do you want to hear my theory?" Marco started.

I rolled my eyes. "Dude, you are *so* drunk."

"No, no, my theory is really good. It's about commitment."

"Already winning material, bro." I put my hand up to call for the check.

"I think commitment is like...a food truck park," Marco ventured. "And let's say, you want a hotdog. Like, the park could have like burgers and ice cream, but no, you want a hotdog. And the park could have tons of hotdog trucks and you pass a few," he relayed carelessly. "Some look really good but you're not quite that hungry yet. So what do you do?" he prompted me.

I blinked at him, blankly. But before I could even attempt to understand where he was going with this, he replied to his own question.

"You keep on walking!" he called out. "I mean you could have been hungry, but not like *hungry*, you know? Then—*finally*—you get to that one food truck. Maybe the hotdogs aren't the fanciest or it could even be the exact same hotdog you passed on the first food truck. But it just hits you, *now* you're hungry." He thumped my back. "And you eat that hotdog, man. You commit to the hotdog because *that's* your hotdog. It's all about timing. And that's when you were ready. That's when you were hungry. And then you leave the food truck park. And then you get married. The end."

I had to shake my head in stifled laughter in disbelief and incredulity. I just patted his back again. "I missed you, man."

"Yes!" Marco exclaimed, standing up to hug me before almost instantly passing out.

***

I sat up in bed, restless, and blew out a breath in frustration.

After having dropped Marco off in his room, literally leaving him on top of his bed, I had gone straight to my room. But I couldn't sleep.

All I could think about was Claire and dwelling on the fact that I knew Claire was in another room. With Wayne.

There was a firm knocking at the door and I straightened up, alerted, my heart already pounding in my chest.

I got up and walked cautiously toward the door but when I opened the door a crack, I saw it wasn't Claire.

It was Alyssa. She was already smiling when she pushed the door open to let herself in. "Hi, Alex."

"Uh, hi, Alyssa," I said with a slight nod.

"Mm." Alyssa pursed her lips, coming up to me to press one hand against my bare chest, making me back up into the room and against the armrest of the leather desk chair. "I've been waiting all day for a chance that we could be alone," she said, before giving me a slight nudge and I plunked into the seat.

I sighed as she unwound her scarf from her neck and put it aside. I knew exactly what she was planning to do. "Um, hey, listen, Alyssa—" I stopped short when she moved to straddle my knee and began to unbutton her coat. "Heeyy, look." I shifted uneasily and put my hand on hers to make her stop, meeting her gaze. "I appreciate what you're trying to do, and I'm really flattered, but—"

Alyssa's face was still bright like she didn't understand what I was trying to say at all. "But what?" she echoed with a devious smile.

That's when I heard a soft knock at the door and my eyes widened when I recognized her voice.

"Hello? Alex? The door is open..."

Claire stopped short abruptly, short of skidding on her heels upon catching sight of us, her jaw dropping instantly in shock.

Alyssa turned to look over at her. She smiled but didn't

move otherwise as she greeted brightly, "Oh, hi, Claire. How's it going?"

Claire blinked a few times, speechless as hell. I saw her take a deep breath, then she met my gaze for a split second before whirling around to bolt.

My heart pounded in my chest again. "Claire! Wait!" I called out, unceremoniously pushing Alyssa off of me before taking off after Claire, grabbing my coat from beside the door as I went.

"Hey—Alex!" Alyssa complained behind me. "Where the hell are you going?"

Claire was already shaking her head when she saw me walking up to her by the elevators. She put her hand up. "Don't."

"Claire." I came closer.

"No, no." She kept shaking her head, still looking in shock. "Don't. Just—just leave me alone."

The elevator doors opened just then and she got on but I followed in after her, clumsily putting on my coat as I let the doors close behind me.

She gave me a desperately exasperated look. "Alex, please."

My frown deepened. "I-I'm sorry—"

For some reason, that earned me a puzzled look from her. "What?"

I cocked my head to one side, studying her expression before it hit me. "I thought..." Obviously, I had thought that the reason she had bolted was that she was jealous of Alyssa being with me. But of course, that wasn't. I heaved faintly in disappointment, at a loss for words. "I..."

She gave me a meaningful look. "This is not about you,

Alex," she told me. "I'm the one with the problem. It's—only just dawned on me what I've become." Her sudden laugh sounded strangled. "I used to be so high and mighty on my pedestal, judging girls like Alyssa for being dumb booty-call girls. And I've only just realized that's exactly what I've been doing." She shook her head. "I am now no different than those floozies," she concluded, looking revolted.

I studied her face intently, aching to comfort her. "Yes, you are. You are totally different," I told her resolutely, wishing I could explain exactly how, if she would let me.

She let out another strained laugh. "I'm sorry but hadn't I just come up to your room about to do the exact same thing as Alyssa? My god, what the hell have I turned into?" Then she dropped her gaze disparagingly. "I have no right to judge any of them," she murmured, pausing as of an afterthought before she added something almost inaudibly. "Or you."

I narrowed my eyes at that but before I could say anything, the elevator doors opened in the lobby.

Claire pushed past me, her eyes wide. She was shaking her head, still looking distraught. "I have to get out of here."

"Claire, come back," I called out, easily catching up to her just outside the hotel doors.

She tried to wave me away. "Just leave me alone, Alex," she snapped, trying to walk faster. "Why are you always around when this shit happens to me anyway?" she wanted to know, sounding frustrated.

I pursed my lips. "Because you need me," I called out.

That finally made her stop short if only to whirl around to shoot me an indignant look.

I blinked, heaving, my heart still pounding in my chest. "I

mean you *need* someone," I amended. "Someone to talk to. A friend." I swallowed, coming closer. "Because...you don't need to be alone with this."

"A friend," she echoed, almost in ridicule. "Are we friends?"

That surprised me a little. "Yes," I answered firmly. "Look," I started after a pause, meeting her gaze evenly. "I know you said this wasn't about me. But maybe the reason I'm always around is because I'm the only one who actually knows what the hell you're talking about. It's something that I happen to be an authority on. I mean, you know as well as I do, *I know* about dumb booty-call girls, more than anyone. So you should believe me when I say—" I raised my eyebrows. "That you are definitely *not* the same as them. You shouldn't even be comparing yourself to any of those girls."

I saw her swallow hard. She didn't say anything but at least I could tell she was listening to me. I gave her a gentle smile. "Look, different people deal with sad things in different ways," I told her. "Sure, you're upset about your ex-boyfriend getting married tomorrow, and the way you decided to deal with it may have been a little unorthodox. But it doesn't mean you're all screwed up. And it doesn't make you a floozy," I concluded.

Claire took a deep breath and I thought I was finally getting through to her, but then she spoke, barely above a whisper, "Oh god, he's really getting married tomorrow."

That made me instantly frown, my chest constricting again, as if somehow it triggered something inside of me, pushing me past the point of sympathy.

It was beyond belief. As in the midst of all of this distress and agony, she was still, and mainly and foremostly, thinking of Marco *freaking* Welling. I mean, for god's sake—was Marco the one out here in the middle of the night trying to console her while she was crying? Has Marco been the one trying to comfort her all this time? Has Marco ever even bothered to ask her if she was okay throughout all this?

"*Jesus Christ*, Claire!" I cursed aloud, annoyed. "When the hell are you going to get over that guy?" I blew out a breath. "Marco loves *Nina*," I told her firmly. "It's *over*. Don't you think you've obsessed about him long enough?"

Claire stared at me, taken aback. I guessed she wasn't used to being told off, let alone be told off by me.

"He's getting married tomorrow. And there's nothing you or I can do about it," I said. "But that doesn't mean it's the end of the world," I told her after a pause. "There's still happiness out there for you. Marco getting married doesn't make that suddenly impossible." I took a deep breath, somewhat tiredly. "And maybe if you unstick your head out of the ground for a split second, you might even see that there *are* other decent guys out there—some even right under your nose."

To which, after another short pause, Claire prompted, "Who, Wayne?"

I blinked, slightly winded. "Yeah. Sure. Wayne." I nodded resignedly, looking away.

Claire and I didn't talk on the way back to the hotel and I didn't walk her to her room. When I got back into my own room, Alyssa was gone. But she had left her scarf on the leather chair.

That night had got to be the strangest night I'd ever had. And in the end, I slept alone.

II

Marco and Nina's Rehearsal Dinner

"Hi, Alex!"

"Hi! Alex, over here!"

"Hey, Alex—"

It wasn't the first time I'd had a barrage of greetings from girls assault me the moment I entered a party, but Marco and Nina's rehearsal dinner was the first time that I didn't feel at all inclined to respond to any of them.

My eyes lit up as I saw Tyler waving and I headed straight over, grabbing a flute of champagne from one of the passing waiters' trays as I went.

"Hey, Alex." Janice gave me a smile as I arrived. Claire was nowhere to be seen yet.

I gave Janice a nod of acknowledgment. "Hey Janice,

looking good," I remarked on her appearance as the three of us headed toward a table.

She tilted her head to one side, looking at me. "Huh, that compliment didn't make me feel as sleazy as normal," she quipped, good-naturedly. "What's going on with you, Alex?"

"I keep telling you, Janice," I told her with a wan smile. "I'm a perfectly decent guy. Honestly," I started, feeling vaguely defensive. "You guys have known me for years. If I really was such an asshole, why do you even bother hanging out with me?"

"Yeah, Jan," Tyler spoke up for me, patting my shoulder as he and I sat down. "Give the guy a break. Weddings must be like Alex's kryptonite."

"Right." Janice nodded wryly, turning to me. "And the next thing you're going to tell me is that you haven't slept with any of the bridesmaids yet." She shook her head in skepticism before going off to mingle some more.

I met Tyler's gaze and he just shrugged. I supposed he could neither support nor contradict Janice's statements either. I was tempted to tell him the truth—that I actually hadn't. Not counting Claire, I hadn't slept with anyone else all week. But I didn't say anything.

I looked over toward Marco and Nina who were greeting guests at the door. They were both beaming, looking like the happiest couple on earth.

I huffed, shaking my head. "So, he's really going through with this," I remarked to Tyler, gesturing to Marco.

"Oh, yeah." Tyler nodded. "What have I been telling you for the last few weeks? Once you find that someone you love, all the doubt stops, and suddenly even the difficult stuff become the simplest things in the world."

I resisted the urge to laugh, not because I found what he said funny, but because I was starting to believe the statement applied to everyone except me. But I just pursed my lips. "Well, you know me," I said dryly. "My whole entire life is just a meaningless quest from one shag to the next." I was meaning to sound facetious and arrogant, except I didn't manage to land it.

"Is that right?" Tyler was watching me carefully. "How's that going, by the way?"

"How's what going?" I glanced up.

"That problem you've been having. You know the one you didn't want to talk about at the bar last week?" he prompted mischievously.

I stopped short, giving him a guarded look.

Tyler grinned. "Look, bro." He thumped on my shoulder. "I just want to make sure you're alright. And that like, no laws are being broken," he added with a chuckle.

I broke a smirk at that. "I'm fine, Ty," I insisted smoothly. "It's all good."

He leaned back in his chair, still looking at me. "Tell you what," he proposed. "If you tell me *right now*, I absolutely guarantee...that I will not tell my wife," he declared. "This is a one-time-only opportunity. If I were you, I'd take advantage of it."

I met his gaze as I considered it.

Maybe I could tell Tyler. He was my friend and I did trust him. He might even have some helpful insights. I certainly was at the end of my rope. And having nobody else to talk to about it for so long was driving me nuts.

After a long pause to think, I tilted my head in a slight nod "fine" and Tyler leaned forward encouragingly.

"There's...this...girl..."

Tyler's eyes widened slightly. It was highly likely that the absolute last thing he thought was that I was having girl problems.

I read his mind. "I know, right?" I prompted, almost unable to believe it myself. I blew out a breath before draining my drink.

He pursed his lips, putting his hand up. "I don't even need to know the rest," he said before giving me an even look. "You need to talk to her. Tell her how you feel."

I shot him a look at how swiftly he turned it around. "It's complicated," I pointed out.

"Bro, it's always complicated."

"No, no, it's *complicated*," I repeated emphatically. "She's with this other guy. And she's still hung up on this other *other* guy. And I know she's just using me. But I guess I'm just not used to being on this end. And I don't want to scare her off. She—she just knows me too well." I shrugged. "Besides, I...don't even know what to say. I—"

Tyler's jaw kind of dropped as he stared at me. "You're already in love with her."

I blinked at him, taken aback. "What? That's—crazy, ridiculous! I mean yeah, I like her, she's really hot but—"

"Mm-mm." He nodded vigorously. "Yep, you don't even realize it. You are in love with this girl, man."

I shot him another look of disbelief. "You don't even know

what's going on," I protested. I refused to believe that Tyler was so enlightened that he had diagnosed my entire situation after a mere five seconds with barely any other information. "You don't even know who she is."

That made him stop short before he raised an eyebrow meaningfully at me. "Would you like me to guess who she is?"

I stopped short myself. "No, please, dear god, don't."

That made him laugh. "Hey look, for what it's worth, you have excellent taste."

"Oh, somehow I don't think *that's* what's in dispute at the moment," I muttered.

"What are you saying? You are Alex *freaking* Keaton. You just have to find that 'deep down' that certain people think you don't have, and *man up*," he said, whacking my chest a couple of times at the same time that someone called for attention by clinking wine glasses to announce that dinner was about to be served.

I stared at Tyler, even as he had begun rubbernecking to catch a glimpse of the food coming out.

Tyler was wrong.

He *had* to be wrong. I wasn't *in love*. Not with Claire. Not with anyone. Surely, that couldn't be the only conclusion. It was ridiculous.

What was all that stuff about evolution again? I was a hunter. I mean, why on earth would I possibly ever want to give up my awesome bachelor life for just one girl?

I felt like I was avoiding absolutely everybody at the wedding rehearsal.

I had almost run into Alyssa and immediately had to turn around, for obvious reasons. Then I almost ran into Marco's unbearably animated cousin Owen, who during all of last night's party kept calling me his "role model" and making comments about how often I must work out. I mean I would have been flattered if he was at least gay.

Trying to avoid Wayne next had made me back up into the curtained-off area where the venue staff made preparations. There were decorative paper chandeliers and extra chairs stacked along the side of the dark room. But through the sheer white curtains, you could still see everything from the brightly lit dining area.

That's how I managed to immediately hide behind a tall shelf of stacked linen before Janice and Claire could see me since I saw them coming from the other side rushing straight for where I was.

I mean I would have let them see me, except I had overheard clearly what Janice was chasing Claire about.

"What do you mean 'with Alex'?" Janice had wanted to know as though she had heard wrong.

Claire stopped in the middle of the room before turning to look at Janice and somehow, I could already guess what was up. And if I had any doubts left over, they were cleared the instant that Janice's eyes popped wide.

"You're kidding me!" she exclaimed in disbelief.

Claire shook her head slowly, her gaze not leaving Janice's face.

"No!" Janice kept exclaiming in a loud hushed voice. "No! You and Alex? No!"

That made me grin as the severity of Janice's reaction was definitely as we'd expected.

Claire shushed her. "Would you keep it down? I'm already regretting having told you."

"Noo..." Janice's face was pale and shocked that I almost laughed out loud but I struggled to stay quiet. "Oh my god," she breathed, a scandal on her face. "Jesus Christ, Claire. How did this happen?"

Claire pursed her lips. "When Marco proposed—"

"Oh my god!" Janice's face cleared up with a realization. "New Year's Eve! Why didn't I see this sooner? Girl, that was totally months ago." Her jaw dropped. "Are you telling me that you and Alex—that you—now—for months?" She couldn't even phrase the entire question.

"Of course not," Claire told her defensively. "It was just that one time." She paused, then caved, grimacing as she went on, "And then a couple times again a few weeks ago." She paused again then wrinkled her nose further. "And last week. And...two nights ago."

I bit my lip. I really should have walked away. But I couldn't pass up the opportunity to get an insight into what Claire thought, especially since I was struggling with everything myself.

But Janice's jaw was still practically on the floor. "Holy shit, Claire! *Oh my god*, you totally have to tell me *everything*. Is he...I mean, is he—really as good as they say?" she wanted to know, still wide-eyed.

I straightened up, eager to hear the response.

Claire just bit her lip and gave Janice this look.

Janice almost yelled out her laughter. "Oh my god! You are going to hell. You are so going to hell! Holy crap!"

I felt as though my grin could not get any wider on my face.

"Shh!" Claire shushed her again. "You absolutely cannot tell anyone. Not even Tyler, do you understand me?" she said firmly.

Janice nodded violently but then she started giggling. "Oh my god, I can't believe he finally went for it—I mean, you. Alex has absolutely no morals whatsoever."

I frowned, a bit slighted by her remark, but Claire spoke up to my defense. "Alex isn't that bad. He's just…dealing with his own problems his own way. And if you think about it, maybe the reason he exclusively goes after dumb booty-call girls is *because* it's easy. And trying to chase after something that might actually be real scares him to death."

In spite of myself, my pulse started to race at Claire's, again, profound analysis. But before I could internalize on it, she went on.

Claire waved her hand. "Anyway, all I wanted to say was that last night, I realized I'd been sort of doing the same thing." She sighed. "I've been holding on to Marco for so long, and especially with this wedding—" She shook her head. "I've only been doing what's easy and holding myself back from finding something real. That's why I've decided that it's finally time to move on. For real this time," she concluded with a nod.

"So, so what? What does this all mean?" Janice prompted. "And what are you going to tell Wayne?"

"Tell Wayne?" Claire echoed.

"Yes." Janice nodded authoritatively. "If you don't really

like him, you shouldn't string him along. You can't just keep using him—*or Alex*—" Then she stopped to reconsider, shaking her head again briskly. "Check that, Alex probably doesn't care anyway."

That made Claire chuckle. "You're probably right about that," she agreed and I felt another frown come on, which deepened further when Claire added, "Wayne's actually pretty great. I like him a lot."

Somehow that stung. I closed my eyes, clenching my jaw as I leaned against the wall, trying not to breathe louder.

"Then you have to end it with Alex," Janice told her. "Either way, you can't keep messing around. I guarantee you, someone is going to get hurt, and I'm just afraid it'll be you."

Claire groaned in frustration, squeezing her eyes shut. "This is all too confusing right now! Can't I just deal with this later?" She made a face as the two of them began to head back toward the party.

"Claire," Janice warned. "The longer you put it off, the harder it'll be. Do it tomorrow," she suggested. "After the wedding."

"Alright, fine," Claire conceded. And the rest of her statement trailed off as they walked out of my hearing range. "I'll do it tomorrow."

Claire was going to end it tomorrow.

It was all I could think of for the rest of the night and I didn't know why but my chest felt heavy. She was going to choose the stable, mature, responsible, I-didn't-even-know-what-he-did-for-a-living-let's-say-architect Wayne, over me,

Alex *freaking* Keaton. And there was absolutely nothing I could do about it.

Ordinarily, that stuff shouldn't be a big deal, least of all, for me. But the insight that I'd so far been afraid to find something real, as well as Tyler's words, kept weighing on my mind. Not to mention all that sudden inside information, and the knowledge that Claire thought I didn't care, was bugging me to hell. Clearly, I had to get to the bottom of this.

While everyone was starting to leave, I noticed Claire across the room, mingling with a few other guests, and neither Wayne nor Janice was anywhere close by.

I set my chin determinedly, my eyes not leaving her for a moment as I walked straight up to her, taking her hand. "Can I borrow you for one second?" I asked, cursorily excusing us from the group.

Up until this point, it was rarely I who initiated anything between us. It had always been Claire. But this time, I couldn't help myself.

I led her away from the party, back toward the staircase, and deftly braced her up against the wall, my lips landing easily on hers.

I kissed her thoroughly, ardently, crushing her body against mine.

She still kissed me back, her arms coming up my chest, around my neck, her fingers in my hair. Her touch was commanding, wanting, insistent, as though she wanted to be as close to me as I did to her.

And everything just melted away. There was no wedding rehearsal. There was no Wayne. No Nina. No Marco.

Just Claire. My Claire.

"Oh Alex," she murmured as I kissed her neck and I shuddered all over again.

It hit me.

Was I in love with Claire?

I loved the way she kissed me, loved the way she looked up at me with those eyes. I absolutely loved the way she ran her fingers through my hair.

Oh shit.

I was in love with Claire? *How in the name of freaking hell did I fall in love with Claire?*

And not just with her body. I had fallen in love with her mind, her spirit. I loved...her kindness, her curiosity, her humor, her always spot-on insights. I loved how bravely if brazenly, she had dealt with her struggles. I loved how strong and confident she was, but I also loved when she was weak.

I felt as though being with Claire made absolutely no sense, but that at the same time it was the only thing in my life that made any sense at all. I didn't want to lose her.

I pulled away briefly, heaving, and I met her lustrous gaze with my heavy-lidded ones. I swallowed hard. "Claire, I..." I started to say, my hand still on the nape of her neck.

But then she whispered, "Let's go upstairs."

At that, I felt a deep twinge of want in my chest. There were no words to describe how badly I wanted to take her up to my room right then. But I stopped when I realized what it was.

This was it. Claire was giving me a send-off.

My chest constricted again. How could it be over already? How could she be ending it? How could I ask her not to? *Could* I ask her not to? I wondered, almost helplessly. And against everything I'd previously held dear, I shook my head. "I'm—I don't think we should. Not tonight. I mean, we'll be very busy tomorrow."

Her arms were still around my neck, her eyes closed as she brushed her lips against mine once more. "Are you sure?" she murmured.

I gritted my teeth, trying not to tremble so damn hard. Her closeness was driving me crazy. It was useless to fight it. And even if I said no, her decision had already been made anyway, and it was too late now, I thought dejectedly.

The only thing I could do, as usual, was enjoy my big win...and move on.

12

Marco and Nina's Wedding

Marco didn't look at all nervous on the day of his wedding. In fact, Tyler was looking more of a wreck as he paced back and forth, worrying about his best man's speech. I watched the contrast between the two of them as I sat on the couch in the groom's room a few hours before the ceremony.

I was already dressed and ready. It wasn't my wedding and I didn't have to make a speech, so there was absolutely no reason for me to be nervous. Besides, it wasn't like things were going to get any better for me.

My chest had felt heavy since I woke up this morning alone in bed.

Last night with Claire had been beyond amazing. And somehow it had felt more intimate than any time I had ever had with anyone ever before.

Given that it was my send-off, I had taken my time. Mostly because I wanted to remember everything about her, but also because I wanted to make it extra special, on the off chance that it was still possible to change her mind about me.

Although between Marco, Janice, and Wayne, let's just say the odds were definitely not stacked in my favor.

Tyler paced anxiously past my nose again. "Ty, seriously man," I had to speak up. "You weren't this nervous on your own wedding day, alright? Settle the hell down."

Marco chuckled as he adjusted his cufflinks. "He's right," he agreed. "Man, does that seem like a long time ago?" he turned to me to ask.

I shrugged nonchalantly. "Three years. Must feel like a lifetime to Ty," I remarked.

Tyler gave me a wan smile as he stopped by me to thump on my shoulder again. "You'll understand soon enough," he said cryptically. "When you find the girl of your dreams, a lifetime is a good thing."

I didn't respond.

Marco just grinned, giving each of us a look. "I'm just glad you're both here," he said, sounding sincere. "Thanks a lot."

"Bro, you'll crush it." Tyler patted his back encouragingly.

"Ahem." Bridgette knocked on the door and the three of us looked up. "Best man." She smiled at Tyler. "And so on." She threw me a plain look before beckoning the two of us over. "Time for usher duties."

"Right." I stood up and Tyler and I headed for the door.

"We'll be right back." Tyler waved at Marco, who mocked a salute at us before we followed Bridgette out and down the hall toward the wedding chapel.

Guests were beginning to arrive. Tyler headed up toward the front of the aisle right away. I was going to be helping seat the guests from the back.

Bridgette shot me a dry look. "It's starting to drizzle outside," she began. "So make sure the guests know where to put their umbrellas and coats."

I nodded, quite amused as I watched Bridgette's expression before she turned to leave.

I guessed that Alyssa had already told her what had happened, or not happened, between us the other night and neither of them was happy about it. But I didn't care. Any other day, I would have been trying to get them to compete against each other for me, using misinformation and jealousy tactics.

Admittedly, it felt kind of unusual not to be strategizing for the best way to do a bridesmaid bingo at a wedding. But maybe Marco had been right. Maybe I was done with the food truck park.

Janice came up the aisle just then and she didn't notice me until I waved in her face.

"Janice." I nodded my greeting briefly.

She stopped, her eyes already popping wide upon seeing me. "Oh. Hi. Alex." She gave me a tentative smile.

I hid my grin. It was all over her face that she was now in possession of some scandalous knowledge about me that she was struggling to keep to herself. "Make sure you have an umbrella if you're headed outside," I told her casually. "Bridgette says it's starting to rain."

"Right." She looked frozen in her spot.

"Did you even know that it rains in Vegas?" I mused,

going on. "It's not supposed to rain in the desert, especially in summer. Did you know that? I mean, *you already know*, right? Right, Janice?"

Janice blinked. "I know nothing!" She put her hands up and took off.

I stifled my laughter then panned my gaze up across the room to Claire, whom I knew was going to be passing out programs near the front. When I saw her my heart began to pound again, but this time not in any sort of anticipation, instead possibly just acute melancholy and frustrated discontent.

She was talking to Wayne, and despite her bright pink bridesmaid's dress, I thought she still looked breathtakingly beautiful. I was almost certain that I was unlikely to find anyone like Claire ever again.

I sighed dejectedly, shaking it off. What was done was done. And I still had to get through this wedding. We both did.

I had just finished seating Marco's great-aunt and was on the way back to the seating chart display when I felt someone tug on my arm. I almost instantly groaned out loud, assuming that it was either Alyssa again, or one of Nina's other over-eager sorority sisters, but when she pushed me through to the adjacent other empty wedding hall, and turned to shut the door, I was stunned when I saw who it was.

"Claire, what—?" I was short of speechless.

"Come here, gorgeous." Claire pulled me closer by my suit lapels, smiling mischievously as she slipped her hands inside my jacket to push it off my broad shoulders, already leaning up to kiss me.

I was absolutely confused. I was expecting a soul-crushing

termination speech. In fact, I was steeling myself for it. But her kiss felt unexpectedly sweet and fiery, I broke off right away.

She stopped, giving me a strange look. "Hey, what are you doing?" she asked lightly, unaware of my change in demeanor.

"I—I can't, Claire..."

She let out a slight laugh. "What are you talking about?"

"I can't—keep doing this with you," I said before I turned away. "Not like this. Not if it doesn't mean anything."

Her forehead creased in puzzlement. "What? What on earth are you talking about?"

I pursed my lips, giving her a meaningful look. "Look, I already know, okay?" I told her. "I know you're going to end it with me. I know you've chosen Wayne. And you know what, you're probably right. Hell, I'm not supposed to care anyway, so just—you don't have to do this. I get it."

Claire had sucked in her breath, her eyes wide. "How do you know about that?"

I made a face. "I...overheard you and Janice talking last night. Sorry."

Her jaw had partly dropped but then she shook her head as if to dismiss it. "Okay," she started after a pause. "Listen, Alex, I—"

I put my hand up. I really didn't want to hear her say it. "Claire, it's fine. It's cool."

"Alex, listen to me," Claire spoke again, her tone firm. "I *wasn't* going to end it."

"What?"

She wrinkled her nose. "I'd only made it seem like I had

decided to. To shut Janice up." Then she rolled her eyes, chuckling. "I mean, you know how she gets."

I felt a smile come to my face as I met her gaze. "So, you're breaking up with Wayne instead?" I asked, amazed.

But then she tilted her head, looking puzzled again. "What? Why?"

And my smile faded again.

Claire noticed and she gave me a slightly exasperated look. "What is going on, Alex?"

I studied her face for a moment, my chest constricting again. "Claire..." My gaze dropped to her mouth and I raised my hand to stroke her lower lip, my pulse already racing, before looking into her eyes again. "I can't stop thinking about you." I sighed, exasperated myself. "And I know it sounds crazy—I mean, *I* thought it was crazy, it's *me*, but I think—I just—I want—" I paused, swallowing hard. "I just want to be with you. Just you...Claire," I declared. "And I want you to just be with me."

She was already looking at me with a seriously bewildered look on her face. And I couldn't even blame her. I probably sounded like a lunatic. But then she started to shake her head. "I don't understand—" Her gaze distracted back toward the door as the organist from Marco and Nina's wedding began to warm up.

I sighed again in frustration. I didn't know how else I could make her understand without being shockingly blunt. I dropped my arms, feeling desperate. "I—I—" I couldn't quite finish.

She was watching me warily. "Alex, I'm not—quite getting the joke. I think uh...maybe we should just get back to the wedding," she suggested, turning to leave, heading out the door.

But I was right behind her. "I'm in love with you, Claire," I burst out.

Claire whirled around, gasping.

Although Claire's alarm seemed less about what I had just said, and more about the one-hundred-and-fifty guests all assembled in the wedding chapel for Marco and Nina's wedding who had all heard, turned to look, and were all now staring at me.

I looked up the front toward the bridal party. Alyssa, Bridgette, Wayne, Tyler, and Janice had all heard me. Janice's jaw had dropped so far, it was almost comical. Then my gaze moved up—and yes, Marco had heard me too. His eyes were wide in surprise and disbelief.

I spun around to meet Claire's gaze but she had turned on her heel and bolted up the aisle and out the exit.

I turned slowly to give everyone a brief sheepish look. "Uh, so sorry to interrupt," I bade politely before I took off after Claire again.

I stopped just outside the doors. Out front was the car park and then immediately The Strip. The light drizzle had already stopped. I looked left and right. Claire was nowhere to be seen. I cursed under my breath, heaving a huge sigh.

"Hey!"

I turned and was surprised to see Marco, looking breathless, coming out the door.

"Uh, hey dude..." I said tentatively.

He put his hand on my shoulder to catch his breath. "What just happened back there?" he wanted to know.

I gave him an apologetic look. "Hey, I'm sorry for causing a scene—"

"No, no, forget about that." Marco dismissed it right away. "Look, did I just hear you say you're in love with Claire?" He looked taken aback.

I met his gaze warily. "Is...that okay?"

"Seriously? With Claire?" Marco looked like he was trying very hard to stifle his laughter and I shot him a narrow-eyed look but he just thumped on my shoulder. "Of course, man, you know? Claire and I—that was super long ago." He shrugged. "And hello? I'm getting married today?"

"Really?" I cracked a small smile.

And I realized that the real reason I had been avoiding asking Marco was because I actually already knew he would be totally fine with it. But I knew if I had his permission, there was nothing holding me back from trying to go after Claire. And the truth was that, deep down, the thought of it actually scared me shitless.

"Sure, but—it's Claire," Marco said, with a tone of ridicule. "I just didn't think someone like you would be into someone like her."

"What do you mean?" I gave him a puzzled look.

He shook his head. "You know," he said. "I always thought women needed to be a certain level of dumb or dirty to get your attention." He grinned. "I just never thought Claire was both."

My eyebrows furrowed in offense as he struck a nerve but before I could respond, Marco said more stuff.

"Then again." He elbowed me, teasing. "No doubt, a man

of your talents would certainly be able to bring the whore out of anyone, am I right?"

I gritted my teeth and before I could stop to think, I reared back to punch Marco in the face.

"Alex!"

I heard Claire exclaim in shock and when I looked over, she was already standing right behind us, though it wasn't clear how much she had seen or heard.

I was also a bit shocked myself, but when I looked over where Marco had fallen down, sprawled on the ground, I noticed, to my great relief, that I had actually missed him. Marco had managed to weave away in time before I landed my punch.

Claire ran up and crouched down beside Marco, looking concerned. "Are you okay?" she asked him.

"What the hell, man? I was just joking." Marco shot me a look of angry disbelief.

I was still heaving. I swallowed hard, trying to rein in my control. I wanted to digest the knowledge that, however in bad taste the joke may have been, Marco had in fact only been joking. But my gaze was pinned to Claire, as she was still bent down beside Marco, holding on to his arm. And if anything, my anger intensified.

After everything that had happened, it was gut-wrenching to realize that my biggest rival wasn't even Wayne after all. It was still, and was always going to be, my best friend. Marco truly was her one weakness.

I gritted my teeth again, my chest constricting sharply.

Tyler came out of the doors just in time to see Claire helping Marco get up, dusting off his pants. "What the hell are you guys doing out here?" He gave each of us a look, except none of us responded.

Tyler just shook his head, before gesturing behind him. "Well, there's about to be a wedding *in here*," he went on, dryly. "And we seem to be missing a few crucial people. The groom, for instance?" he prompted, looking at Marco.

Marco was shaking his head at me. "Dude, you need to settle down." He brushed off his suit some more. "Take five, or take a walk or something and sort out your shit," he ordered. "This is supposed to be the happiest day of my life."

Tyler directed Marco back into the wedding hall and I could only watch as he walked in, Claire still on his arm with Tyler following suit.

I turned my back, squeezing my eyes shut in exasperation. *How the hell did I get here?* I blew out a breath, raking my fingers through my hair.

I had almost ruined Marco's wedding.

I had lost Claire.

I never had Claire... I told myself, cursing under my breath again. I seriously needed to calm down.

I was stalking moodily across the parking lot, headed toward the street to take a walk to clear my head when I heard footsteps right behind me.

"You're a complete psycho, do you know that?" Claire declared out loud, her breathing labored.

I stopped, standing with my back to her, a deep frown on my face.

Honestly, if I heard another word about how awesome Marco was compared to me and how she couldn't manage to get over him, I was seriously going to walk in front of a bus. I had to roll my eyes. "I'm sorry!" I barked loudly.

"Alex, look at me. We need to talk."

I didn't turn around but Claire started anyway.

"Look, I'm not sure what's going on with you," she said. "And I don't understand why you suddenly seem to be taking Marco's wedding worse than I am. But...if you want to take back what you said to me—back there, I—"

"I don't," I cut in brusquely.

I heard her sigh out loud. "Then I *really* don't understand." She dropped her hands resignedly. "I thought we were both just having fun. I thought—I thought—"

"What do you want me to say?" I threw up my hands exasperatedly, still not looking at her. "That the last few weeks with you have been perfect? That I've never had so much fun with anyone else in my entire life? That I know it sounds ridiculous but I want you to give me a chance?"

She paused. "Is that what you want to say?"

I stiffened. "Not if you're still in love with Marco," I remarked and when she didn't refute it, my chest constricted again. I took a deep breath. "Look, you were right about me. I *have* been afraid to find something real too, for too long. But I also know I'm right that you deserve better than Marco. And Wayne." I shrugged pointedly. "Well, he's clearly not good enough for you. I mean, what does the guy even do for a living?"

At that, I heard Claire chuckle. "Something with computers."

"Great." I groaned, shaking my head. *Stable* and *lucrative*.

"So...what you're saying is, you think *you're* good enough

for me," she stated, her tone literally somewhere between amused and bemused.

I was still shaking my head. I heaved another sigh before I turned to meet her gaze. "I'm saying—I'm better...now. Being with you has made me...better than good enough." I gave her a steady look before starting. "I've been hearing a lot of theories lately. And I don't really know if this is love," I admitted. "It could be, or it could also be something else. All I know is I'd like to give it a try," I paused meaningfully. "If it's with you."

Claire was studying the storm brewing in my eyes intently, quietly.

I searched her face. "Has it really never crossed your mind? Not even once?" I asked, both dreading and anticipating her response, and my chest felt tight at her prolonged silence.

"Say something," I pressed apprehensively.

Then after a long while, Claire broke a soft smile, a sudden clarity in her blue eyes as she gazed up at me. And all she said was, "Yeah...I'm definitely not in love with Marco anymore."

And I started to smile myself, in relief, in hope, in such elation that I wanted to kiss her right then and there, but before I could grab her neck and pull her toward me, someone yelled out from behind us.

"Are you two done yet or what?"

When I glanced over, I was surprised to see Janice poking her head out of the door from the wedding chapel. She was waving the two of us over urgently. "The bride and groom are waiting, you guys," she called out pointedly from across the car park, her volume carrying surprisingly well.

But after a beat, she just rolled her eyes. "Whatever. If you're not back inside in two minutes, we're doing this thing without you," she warned before disappearing back through the door.

I had to laugh. Claire was also laughing when she met my gaze again. "So uh, what do you want to do now?" I asked.

Claire's smile turned somewhat devious as she regarded me with a look. "I think I've had enough of Marco and Nina," she remarked. "You wanna get out of here?"

I couldn't bite back my grin. "Absolutely," I replied with full conviction. I could not have thought of anything better. "You want to go get some coffee? I thought I saw a Starbucks around the corner."

And Claire smiled back. "That sounds good."

I let out another slightly nervous chuckle, starting to walk down the street.

"I still can't believe you tried to hit Marco on his wedding day," Claire commented casually, falling into step beside me.

I made a face. "It's not like I planned it. It was a reflex."

"Sure it was," she mused in ridicule.

"What? He was being an asshole," I said defensively. "He basically implied that you were dumb and dirty and that I've somehow turned you into a whore—," I relayed and I saw Claire's eyes pop in outrage.

"He said *what* now?" Her eyes blazed in fury. "Imma freaking hit him too!" she exclaimed, turning on her heel to march back toward the wedding chapel.

But I laughed out loud, catching her arm and pulling her toward me instead. I gazed down at her, unable to stop smiling before I started to lean my head down closer to hers.

Claire blinked up at me. "What, you're going to kiss me— out here in public, on the street?" she asked, surprised.

I gave her a look. "Who's going to stop me?"

That made her smile widen before she replied, "Absolutely nobody."

***

The End.

Don't miss a happy ending!

SARA BELLCAMP writes offbeat, quirky romance. She mainly writes sweet romance under the pen name **Sara Breaker**. Simple, sweet stories and all the happy endings.

She lives in New Zealand with her husband and two kids. Suburban mum by day and author by night, she loves to live vicariously through her characters. They don't have to vacuum all day long and are always guaranteed happy endings, no matter how melodramatic she writes them.

She likes binge-watching TV shows and reading books that take you through the requisite ups and downs of a good story, breaks your heart, puts it back together, bam! happy ending—but then still have enough time to wash the dishes after.

Join her mailing list now and get a FREE e-book!

https://subscribe.breakerworlds.com/romance

Other Titles by Sara Breaker

Sara's Sweet Romance

Young Adult Sweet Romance
The Perfect Deal
The Real Thing
Just an Alternate
Change of Mind

New Adult Sweet Romance
Insert Happy Ending
Holiday Blues

Hale Valley Sweet Romance series
Switch on Christmas (a prequel novella)
Crushing On You

Sneak Peek

Insert Happy Ending

Ten years after high school, the most popular jock and the biggest nerd meet again by coincidence. Ben and Marga take a shot at the chance they might've already missed. And you can probably guess the rest. Or can you...?

***

"I'm sorry," Marga apologized again. "I just have no idea what to talk about. I mean, with *you*."

Ben stopped midway from raising his drink to his mouth to ask, "What do you mean?"

Ironically (or obviously), they'd had no more sessions in common for the rest of the day, but when they had met up at lunch, Ben had somehow managed to coerce Marga into skipping the day's last training session. He'd half meant it as a test. Back in school, Marga would have been the last person he'd have thought would ever skive off class.

But Marga's personality was different from what he would have thought. All he had anyway were stereotypes and fragments of hearsay. But she wasn't timid, she wasn't quiet, she wasn't boring. And he'd just figured out why she had been talking about the weather for the last half hour.

Marga gave him a plain look. "Come on," she started. "We

haven't seen each other in like ten years, and even then we—"
She broke off.

"We what?"

"We weren't technically friends," she pointed out. "And...you're—*you*." She gestured to him as if it was a bad thing before her voice lowered to a hush. "Are you even aware that all the women in this room would kill to be sitting in my chair right now?"

Ben raised his eyebrows. He was used to the flattery. Of course, he was. But the way Marga did it. She was just so...*frank*. He let out a chuckle, somehow feeling self-conscious. "I—don't notice that stuff anymore," he lied, not meeting her gaze. "I've got a girlfriend." He shrugged.

Marga gave him an incredulous look, but he already knew she wouldn't buy that. "You're Ben Hamilton. Everyone knows who that is," she said. "I bet you're still not really 100% sure who I am."

"Uh..." Ben tried to figure out how to respond. She was absolutely right and he knew there was no way he could get away with pretending otherwise.

She pursed her lips knowingly as if reading his mind, but she went on. "You must have known, back then you couldn't sneeze without the whole school knowing about it," she told him. "People posted bulletins of your football stats and every injury you ever got. I happen to know each and every detail of your first date with Andrea. And I'm probably not supposed to tell you this, but I have friends who had photos of you in their locker—" She stopped short, realizing she was rambling. "Sorry, that's sort of embarrassing to say," she finished, coloring slightly.

The stories made Ben laugh. "Look, Marga," he started, hoping he sounded rational. "High school was a lifetime ago. I just think we...shouldn't be stuck with who we used to be, you know? I know I'm not that guy anymore. I'm sure you wouldn't want people to think you were still the same person back then, right?"

***

Enjoyed the preview? **Insert Happy Ending** is also available to purchase at your favorite online bookstore.

Sneak Peek

Holiday Blues

Snowed in at school over Christmas. What else is there to do? Maybe fall in love with the guy you least expected? Too bad he's dating your roommate...

***

I stopped in the doorway of our room. It was still a horrendous mess, especially Wanda's side that I wouldn't have been surprised if there was a family of mice already living under the piles of laundry.

But my stomach was churning at what Becca from downstairs had just told me.

Apparently, I had missed a call from Jason.

Because I was out all morning with Lachlan.

Wanda's boyfriend.

I buried my face in my hands. What the heck was I doing?

I was getting a crush on my roommate's boyfriend.

I flopped facedown onto my bed with a groan, pushing aside near-empty packets of potato chips with a loud crinkle.

It was rationalizing time.

Of course, I would get a crush on Lachlan. Given this morning's commotion, every other girl in our building probably already had a crush on him too.

He was sweet. He was cute. He was crazy smart. He had the most adorable smile ever.

I shook my head briskly to clear it, checking back in with reality.

It was fine. Everything was fine. Everything was alright. This was completely normal.

Besides, nothing happened. Nothing was *going* to happen.

Also given what Wanda was probably doing with Doug, it wasn't even entirely clear whether Wanda would care at all anyway.

Still... I guessed I could understand where Wanda was coming from.

She had barely seen or heard from her boyfriend for so long, and sometimes when you don't see someone, maybe you forget what they're like.

I frowned against my sheets before pushing up on my elbows in exasperation, casting a dull glare around the room.

This mess totally needed to be cleaned.

***

Enjoyed the preview? **Holiday Blues** is also available to purchase at your favorite bookstore.